SOUTH
TEXAS
TWIST

To Rachel & Chad

Enjoy my Book and
The Ables Chairs

Tony Molina

Tony Molina Publishing • 2018

South Texas Twist

ISBN-13: 978-1-7325294-0-3

Published by Tony Molina, LLC

www.529books.com
Editor: Lisa Cerasoli with Adrian Muraro
Cover Design: Claire Moore
Interior Design: Lauren Michelle

This book is dedicated to Susan Rawlings Molina. She taught me to be true to myself and showed me the importance of getting out of my own way. Her guidance and inspiration have been invaluable to my writing career.

SOUTH TEXAS TWIST

PROLOGUE

The Yucatan sun stings like a rub from a jellyfish. I can't believe the heat pounding on my back as I lay here on the Mexican beach. I really thought the South Texas heat was bad, but this, not even Tarzan could stand. My eyes crack open just enough to catch a glimpse of a sand crab four inches from my face—next to all these empty Indio beer bottles that somehow got left out here by who knows who. Oh my god, I see everything in metro-color. I look for a tourniquet for my bloodshot eyes.

As I begin to focus, I can see a Patron Roca tequila bottle lying by me—empty, of course. Now I understand why I hate tequila. I can't believe my crew just left me outside in the sand to bake. Thank god I have a permanent tan or I'd have third-degree burns. We Texicans can't burn, it's a law.

Two weeks of R&R is about all I can stand. Time to get our minds right, go back to Texas, and start our new positions as lead players. After all we went through, we're going to jump right back into the fire with both feet. But right now, I have to get to my feet without passing out. The sand is level to the ocean, with mounds of seaweed in the way like a wall to protect us.

Standing up is not a given, but I still have the chops to pull an all-night pachanga. As I focus on the seaweed, I can see an arm sticking out of the mounds. Are we getting hit? Are we on the dangle out here in the open? Who could find us out here in the sticks? Well, that did it; I begin the quick walk to the mounds of seaweed and see the arm has tattoos. Damn, they got Jay. They left him in the weeds as a message. As I get closer, I can see the rest of his body is still attached.

I pull the weeds off Jay's face and realize he is dead—dead drunk. Pinche puto jerkoff scared the shit out of me.

"Jay, you okay, brother?"

Jay turns and hugs the mound of seaweed like it's a broad.

That's it. We are going back home to face the real world, and I mean today.

I stroll back into the beautiful, two-story house we have been relaxing in after our fiasco in Nuevo Laredo. I see Paco making migas and eggs. Rigo is chopping jalapeños, tomatoes, and cilantro for a pico de gallo salsa.

"Okay, everybody, pack your shit. We are on the hunt back home."

Paco drops the spoon and Rigo gives me the "it's about time" look.

"Rigo, please go get Jay out from the weeds so we can get the hell out of paradise."

THE RETURN

S lowly driving down this dusty ranch road with the window down in this old Chevy is not my idea of a good time.

Rigo will not shut up about it. "It's hot, Toño, speed it up."

"You know why we have to drive slow and why the windows are down."

"I know, but what else am I going to bitch about?"

"I swear, Rigo, I'm going to throw you out of this car and you will be on the stroll all the way back to Zapata."

"Stop!" a voice yells from the backseat. I hit the brakes deep in this South Texas wilderness, where the cactus and mesquite trees work overtime to stay alive.

In the distance, we see a Border Patrol car hauling ass to cut us off from the sendero road we are about to get on. The problem is he has one fence to open before he crosses our path, and we are aware and waiting. About the time the Border Patrol agent hits his brakes to open the fence, Paco utters from the backseat, "EPP."

Rigo and I immediately cover our ears and brace ourselves. All we hear next is the crack of the .308 cal. Between one and two seconds later, we see the dust fly by the Border Patrol car.

"Paco, did you hit the mark?" I ask in a whisper.

"No, man, hold on. EPP."

We slap our hands across our ears again and Paco shakes out another round.

"I hit it, I got it, putos!"

"Finally." Rigo pops up and the fight is on.

"Cut it out, Rigo, he hit the mark. It's a 600-yard shot." It's better than we can do.

Paco starts in, "It's an 800-yard shot, Toño, and it happened to be a six-inch target I had to hit. Excuse me for hitting the wheel an inch away from the tire."

We all start laughing and watch Border Patrol pull his peashooter out and hide behind his car. He must love his family, because he is not going to move from that spot until we are long gone.

"Now, can we raise the windows and turn the air on, please?"

"You know why we keep the window down?"

"Yes, because we don't want to pay for any more car windows when Paco fires his long rifle."

"And?" I press him.

"Because we will be hearing that ringing sound for the rest of the afternoon like last time."

"Attaboy, cowboy."

"Vamonos, and let's get this load to the ranch so they can fly it out of here."

"Toño, where is it going to this time?"

"Chingado, Rigo, don't ask those questions. Not even between us. Not our business." Since we got back from Yucatan, it has been very hush-hush between us and the Mexican Cartel. Forget about even talking to El Commandante. "We did kidnap his daughter right from under

3

his nose and played him and Mexico like a trompo. But why hold a grudge? We work for both of them."

"What do you mean by that, Toño?" Paco asks.

I'm not sure. "One thing I do know is that we have to get this load to the ranch and out of here before la jura calls in the bird and tracks us before we get it in the air."

"Got it, boss."

Back on point. These guys never cease to amaze me. They can go from hot to cold in the blink of an eye. That's why they're my crew.

We pull into a ranch way east of Zapata, closer to Hebbronville and a whole new set of problems arise. A small Cessna Skywagon is sitting by a dirt runway, blades barely turning. We pull up and this bald, tattooed gangster jumps out of the plane and starts walking toward me. You know the type—saggy, khaki pants, white t-shirt and Chucks, and a really dark attitude. Like he could die right there and not give a shit. He walks right up, knowing Paco and Rigo are halfway to pointing their weapons at him. He doesn't care. He has that head-back, glazed-eyes, lowrider look. But not like Pachuco Jay. This guy doesn't have the stones to sell the look.

I pop my Cold Steel knife in my right hand and hide it behind my thigh. Let's see what this big city boy has for us river rats.

"Orale," he stammers out. "You speak English?"

"I don't know," I tell him. "You speak Spanish?"

This low-level, hard, city-dwelling gangster thinks he can fly down in his piece-of-shit '70s Cessna and play big dog in our town?

"I'm here to pick up the shit we paid for up front last week. Now, where is it, puto?"

"Okay, whachale nalgas chorriadas pajaro nalgon—this is my town, so you tone it down and you might get your shit."

"You don't know who I am, ese, do you?" this numbskull asks.

"I know who you are. You're the chump in the woods by your lonesome. You're unarmed and begging for the shit you were stupid enough to pay for up front. That's who you are, so just stand there, shut up, and we will allow you to leave with your shit."

This guy is crazy, but not stupid. He played his card and got trumped. It helps to have Paco pointing his .308 and smiling at him the whole time.

"Just give me my shit," he spits out without the same vigor in his voice.

5

I head wave Rigo, and he brings up two duffle bags and drops them in front of this gangster. We both back up to the car and vamoose.

We leave this cat standing in a middle of a ranch with two duffle bags by his feet.

You can tell this guy is pissed. I knew he was a punk, because as soon as we got far enough away, he began to motherfuck us and throw gang signs. Something didn't sit right with me about this guy, the plane, or maybe his attitude. It felt more like an audition for a bigger play. I have a bad feeling we will see this lowrider again.

BIG NOISES IN THE VALLEY

Ever since we returned from our Yucatan excursion, the Mexican Cartel has been keeping a close eye on us for a very good reason. They're hard-pressed to fully trust an outfit that beat them at their own game. They never call on any type of phone—only pagers to pass along the meeting information on loads they need shipped or any special piece of work they need done, along with a timeline. Smart way to do business in today's high-tech surveillance world. They go high, we go low on the South Texas battleground.

Driving away from that cholo vato uptown city boy, I just couldn't shake this dark feeling I might end up regretting the way I slapped the traveler down like a little bitch. The dice are rolling, and I'm just not sure who is doing the tossing.

Rigo is sitting in the front seat that's usually reserved for his big brother. Paco stays in the backseat, clings to his long rifle like a sixteen-year-old hugs his first girlfriend. Looks kind of fucked up the way he rubs and caresses that rifle. If he kisses it, I'm throwing him out of this piece-of-shit Nova.

"Toño, where do you think that puto is from? Houston? Dallas?"

"No, Paco, that cat had Fort Worth tattooed all over him."

"Bullshit! How you know that?"

"Rigo, did you even look at his tats?"

"I saw them all."

"Did you? Did you really check out the laughing and crying masks? The RI tattooed inside the diamond on his neck, or the Funky Town tats across his throat?"

"Funky Town, what's that?"

"You need to get out of the sticks, Rigo. Funky Town is what they call Fort Worth."

"Ah, you're a smart mofo, Toño."

"Paco, you know I've dropped off chingos of shit in Fort Worth. It is an Old West town. Dude, they used to have real, no-shit Capone gangsters."

Fort Worth used to have an area around Jacksboro Highway where Chicago and New York ran gambling and whores. They did the Bogart shit—fedoras, suits, and Tommy guns. It was said you could find the bodies lying in the middle of the street, riddled with bullets like Bonnie and Clyde (who did hang out there, by the way). Turf wars a go-go, baby.

"Yeah, but this guy looked like just a crazy cholo."

"Rigo, that cat didn't care about shit. He didn't care about being outmanned or outgunned. He's what we call a wild card with nothing to lose."

"Well, good riddance to that city boy. We will never cross paths with that dude."

"I hope you're right, Paco. I just have that rock-in-my-gut feeling we will see him again."

"Ya, hombre, let's go get a chicken fried steak and a beer. We earned it."

"Did we, Paco?" It took you two shots to hit that Border Patrol's tire.

And the fight was on like *Donkey Kong*.

3

CHICKEN FRIED HEARTBURN

I don't like the drop and roll with the Funky Town cat, but what the fuck.

When we get to town, we have the best chicken fried restaurant in Texas and, to be bold, the world. This place has been a staple in our little Zapata for over thirty years, give or take a lie or two. As you drive up the gravel parking lot, you can smell the fried steak penetrating the air. I mean, there is not a place like this restaurant anywhere in South Texas. It's a standalone building, whitewashed about 100 times, with no windows, just a front and back door we have all used for many different reasons.

We drive around the restaurant, checking all the cars and trucks in the parking lot. You never know who or what agency might be eating at this joint. Even cops can find the best food in town, as long as it's free or half price.

Well, it's a small lunch crowd with all local plates. As usual, we park by the back door, facing out for a quick dash if needed. We never leave anything to chance. Cut the fat from every problem, and you will live longer in our business.

"Paco, trunk the rifle and hurry, cause I'm hungry."

"You're always hungry, bro."

We walk in and we are the faces. Wave and nod to everyone and head to our favorite table. Lupita walks up and, as usual, asks with her sweet voice that hasn't changed since high school, "Do you ever sit at any other table?"

"Lupita, we love you, don't we, guys."

"Ya, Toño, quiero refinar."

Lupita looks right at Rigo. "The usual for all you guys?"

I nod as Rigo and Paco fight over bread and butter she just set on the table.

Have you ever been by a dog or horse and suddenly they stop and look in a specific direction? I just had that feeling the way Paco was peering behind me.

He nods and murmurs, "Trooper."

"Reed?"

"EPP."

I can sense he's getting closer by the sound of his shiny, black, leather gun belt rubbing on his belt keepers.

Without turning, I blurt out, "Reed, how's the racecar coming along?"

Reed got dumped in the town years ago for something he did somewhere like Corpitos (Corpus Christi) or Robstown. Anyway, we leave him alone and he leaves us alone. He writes his tickets and works the highway accidents, and we coexist like whiskey and wine. Reed loves anything that goes fast. Your chances of outdriving him are slim to none. He is the best wheelman around. Too bad he doesn't fiddle with the dark side.

The story goes he built a hotrod Chevy Vega with slick, oversized back tires. Nothing street legal about this car. He took it out where he lives, hit the gas pedal, and the damn car spun three times around, sideswiping his take-home black and white DPS car. Explain that to your commander. Reed will be with us until he retires.

He leans in and whispers, "I heard a Border Patrol was fired on earlier today by the river. I also heard it was a 500-yard shot that disabled his cruiser. You wouldn't know anything about that, Toño?"

I can see Paco dying to correct Reed's yardage miscalculation. "Yeah, I did it. You planning on arresting the criminals?" As I stare into his eyes, his grin shifts. Just like that, he looks blank, dull.

With the little dignity he has left, Reed stands up straight and calmly asks, "How are the chicken fried steaks today?"

I smile.

He walks off, sitting in his usual corner table for one.

You can't show fear in South Texas. The sharks smell blood in the sun around here.

We ate our chicken fried steaks with the choice of white or brown gravy. I'm bothered by Reed's ballsy comment. He knows something I don't. Something's not right in the air today. If there is a play, I better find out.

A CHAT, THEY SAY

L ife has a way of doing its thing without any help from me. I drop my boys off. They have been quiet as mice. Once you feed the tigers, they rest. This is the main reason we never feed until the task is done.

Driving home through Zapata on Highway 83, the sense of home strikes me. The heat fries off the highway, and the hot air burns your eyes, even through the squinting. I belong to this rough land, and sometimes, belonging is enough. Calmness hits me.

Just when I begin to settle into the things I have done and the person I have tried to change into, real life hits. My pager begins to rock, and I see the Mexican Cartel wants to have a chat in Guerrero, Mexico in two hours. They don't need a response. It was not a question, but an order.

Since we played out our last hand against the Mexican Cartel and El Commandante, everyone's found out about our drag move, the talk with the German, and my tio's Houdini move. They have kept us working, constantly checking up on us, double-counting the money, and weighing whatever "product of the week" we are responsible for transporting. For the past six months, it has been small-time stuff. Pickups, drop offs, no major pieces of work.

I'm thinking it's about time to bring us in as family or kill us as liabilities. I'm not sure which one, but it's coming.

I have to go to this meet alone. It would be useless to bring any of my crew as backup. "One riot one ranger," as the Rinches used to say.

Guerrero is thirty minutes south of Zapata, across the Falcon Bridge over the Rio Grande. As kids, my jefe would take the family to Guerrero to buy meat, cokes, and have a dinner on the cheap.

I'm going to this meeting blind. I can't call anybody for a heads-up on who or what will be waiting for me. I can't shake the feeling I have from the meet with the Funky Town gangster, or how he eyeballed me with more curiosity than fear. I hope this meet has nothing to do with that city slicker.

I head home to feed my dogs and give my maid a heads up on where I'm going and who to call if I don't come back in twenty-four hours. I scare the shit out of her but, I have to say, I get a kick out of it. I do ham it up a bit.

As I pull off the highway and head west toward my chante, the dogs are barking and the heat even has the cactuses bowing. Its 110 degrees in the shade; not even the devil could stay out in this. I have this cool Spanish hacienda with a ten-foot electric gate.

Rule one: pull in just far enough to let the gates close right behind your truck. I had a cousin that let two killers follow him inside his gates and he got peppered with bullets. Hence, I have this beautiful house now. I did pay his widow for the hacienda with Chinese arithmetic, one lump sum. She was happy to haul ass back to San Antonio. Maybe I will see her again at her old job working at the Coyote Ugly bar in Downtown San Antonio.

All clear around the patio, and the dogs are waiting to get fed. Time to get my mind right and face the Mexican Cartel—

or Raptors, as I like to call them, since our last little dance on the South Texas drag. When you are eyeball to eyeball, you really have to watch your six and three and nine. They adapted and learned this new technique from who knows who, but it worked. I think one of their boys must have read a book or something.

They used to come right at you, and it seemed more respectful like that, face to face, like the Civil War days. Now, they have become backstabbers. They have lost their honor and are losing support from the people, which keep the cartel safe and protected by not ratting them out.

I know there is not a big distinction on how you kill—dead is dead—but it does mean a lot when dealing with people of honor and respect. You start losing respect, you will do anything, like a rabid dog on the street. Yeah, people fear you, but they won't think twice about putting you down.

I prepare for the worst. I will have to cross the bridge at the Falcon Dam and then head into Guerrero, Mexico. Hell, most of the Immigration and Border Patrol guys on that bridge are from Zapata, anyway. Who else would want to live there? It's a hardship location, so all the South Texas guys take the jobs. You might think this is a good thing, but a red flag pops up when I cross the river: a known smuggler with known ties to the Mexican Cartel. Phone calls are made on both sides of the border. If I had to slide in unannounced, I would boat in unnoticed, but because it's just a meet without pickups or swaps, I will go right through the front door.

I will leave my Glocks and boot gun in my safe and grab my Cold Steel and belt knife. I give them a quick look, check the smoothness and sharpness of both blades. Don't want to get jammed up and have my blade lock up over dirt or lint. Trust me, it can and does happen.

Always check your wares. You want your edges so sharp that if Pancho Villa himself popped up, he would enjoy a slice from your Cold Steel.

I have psyched myself up into a frenzy and placed my dead eyes on the stare. This is hard to describe. It's like a camera lens that locks between a snap, frozen and lifeless. It's also called the thousand-yard stare, or the "I don't give a shit" stare. To sell it, they have to think you have a motive behind the fearless attitude. So, basically, you want them to think you're a badass with something up your sleeve.

My biggest problem is what to wear to this soirée. I jump in the shower and use my Pureology shampoo, which really works with my greasy hair. Having Aztec blood is groovy, but it comes with oily hair, which can suck, and a warrior attitude, which doesn't.

Clothes-wise, I will have a dilemma. What should I wear to a meet in a shithole Mexican town with Raptors? There is only one way to dress in this turd hunt: Short-sleeve psycho bunny black t-shirt. V-neck, of course. Robert Graham blue jeans with a pair of Vince perforated sneakers with white soles. And to tie all this together, a pair of Polo orange socks with green stripes, bam! Always overdress; it throws short-minded, pointy-boot-wearing Mexican killers off their game.

As I walk out to my King Ranch truck, I look back and hope I don't end up like my cousin. It would really piss me off to see Paco or Rigo living in my casa. But, hey, what are you going to do?

This life we hated at first, we've learned to embrace. Funny how things work out when you become the boss. My tio was a rough asshole, but he taught me well. Knowing he's still on the lam somewhere with that fat Machete gives me hope I might still be around at his age. I know it's fucked up thinking this way, but what choice do I have—abandon the flag and flee the fort? Flee where? Wait for the cartel to catch up and make us an example of what happens to soldiers who dare cross them? I'll keep that in the back of my mind on this meet.

No time for pity or fear; it's time to take the snapshot and drill my dead eyes.

I pull out and wait for the gate to close behind my truck, just in case.

As I pull out onto Highway 83 on my thirty-minute drive to the bridge, I'm racking my brain about this meet. They aren't going to kill or torture me because I have no information they need. And what about that tattooed clown from Funky Town?

Made my turn at the Falcon Lake Dam toward the US checkpoint.

Shit, it's Ramiro working the bridge. "Ito," as we call him. We go back a ways. As kids, we would go out and shoot everything in sight at the Oso Blanco Lodge with his .410 shotgun. We were close all through elementary and junior high. But everything changed when my tio took me under his wing. I shifted to smuggling, and Ito went the way of immigration. Can't have crooks as friends if you want a job with La Jura (the law).

He hasn't changed a bit. He still has that ugly beard that he's had since the fifth grade. Short, pudgy, with those weird, green eyes that are few and far between down here. Ito should have been a comedian. He doesn't try to be funny, but he takes off on these tangents about your mom and the bus driver in the backseat—blah, blah, blah—and it's funny as shit. I do miss my friend, but decisions we make do affect other people, especially the ones we love.

21

I pull up to Ito and it starts.

"Hijo de la chingada, pinche puto bastardo, no vales la verga que te meti anoche." How you doing, Toño?

"It's all good, Ito." We have a laugh—our weird, ritualistic greeting.

"What and where are you going?"

"I'm just going to Guerrero to buy cheap meat and Carta Blanca beer for a party I'm throwing. I'd invite you, but it's all about work. You know how it is, my brother from another mother."

"Toño, cut the shit out before you run out of luck, vato."

"Brother, I'm always working on that. Say hello to your jefitos, will you. Not your pinche brother—kick him in the ass for me."

"I would, but he lives in the big city of Laredo Todo Mammon.

Toño, go through, but I'm going to strip your truck on the way back, so you know."

"I know, Ito, it's part of the job, my friend. Hey, Ito, te vañas nalgas chorriadas."

Ito laughs and waves me through. He knows the game, as we all do. Off to the Mexican immigration entry, where all I get is a half-assed wave. And just like that, I'm back in the devil's backyard. I hope he has no interest in me today.

THE GERMAN

D riving into Guerrero is like taking a trip back in time. Rocky dirt roads and old shacks. I slow down for the horse and wagon hauling tires to god knows where. The buildings all have faded paint, like it was slapped on back in the 1800s and no one's bothered to touch it up since. Old, green and white pitted walls that have seen time pass by, like an old woman talking about the horse and buggy days as she sits in a new car.

I get to the downtown of Guerrero, which has the only paved street in the whole shitty town. It's 3:00 p.m., and all the bodegas—pool halls—are open after siesta time. If you drive by around noon, all these stores are closed.

The page I was sent says: *Pelotas.* I pull up into the "parking lot" next to it. "Parking lot" is a fancy word for "this field of grass and trash next to the pool hall," but it is what it is. Pelotas is named after a well-known whorehouse in Nuevo Laredo. The late owner of that establishment was known as Pelotas, which means balls. I usually get met with some Cartel hey boy and follow them to wherever they feel safest, so that's what I'm waiting on.

Shit. A new, black Suburban pulls up behind my truck and stops. Well, they think they have me. Rule two: never get behind a truck—you will get run over. I have my truck running with my foot on the brake, ready to shift into R, hit the gas, and drill them to the river if I have to.

I see the passenger door open and I immediately feel better. I don't know this cat, but if it were a hit, they would have sent someone I know or even trust. There aren't many. This Mexican is wearing a god-awful red shirt with two bull riders embroidered on each shoulder. He's about twenty-five years old, with short, black hair and gray dress pants. I couldn't make this up if I wanted to. I keep waiting to see a midget and a fat, bearded lady exit behind him. Fucking circus-dressed clown.

As he gets to the bed of my truck, I open the door.

He stops dead in his tracks.

I whisper, "Bueno, ora que." He must be a new guy, but he isn't stupid.

"Ven con nosotros."

"Para donde?"

"El Aleman quiere ablar con tigo."

Holy shit, the German himself wants to have a powwow with me. What game is afoot? I slowly step out, close and lock my truck. I walk up to the red shirt and whisper, "Cuida la troca loco."

He smiles and pats me down. He takes my knives and leads me up into the front seat of the Suburban.

Sitting in the hit seat is not a comfort. More people have been killed in the front passenger seat because you're out of position for fight or flight.

I snap at the red shirt, "Sientate atrás del choffer."

He slides away from behind my seat, then looks out the window with a smile and chuckle. If I have to sit in the hit seat, I'm shaving the odds to my favor. Now, I can keep an eye on bullfighter boy and the driver.

At first glance, the driver looks uninterested in the happenings. He looks to be in his forties, trim, wearing yellow Ray Ban shooter glasses with the ear wrap. Most squares won't think anything about this, but the German is in town, and these yellow shooting glasses with a ring in the middle are rare, expensive, and in demand by people who shoot a lot. This guy is the one to watch. If he moves, it will be for a purpose. Another dead giveaway are the cargo pants and Hi-Tech black boots. This guy is here to look me over, I bet.

Damn German takes no chances, especially after the South Texas drag we did. I know he was impressed, because he has one of his main boys babysitting me right now. The chump in the back is only a distraction. Let's play with this merc a little.

I place both hands on the dash in front of me, palms up, and look at him with a smile. I whisper, "Feel better, slick?"

The driver doesn't even turn to face me. He just cracks a hint of a smile and relaxes a smidgeon. He knows I made him, but I have to respect whatever he has tucked by his left side.

I turn to Rodeo Boy in the back. "Quida mi filas, las quiero patras pallaso." I look at the driver. "It's a Cold Steel Voyager with a tanto serrated blade. You know what I'm talking about."

The driver nods, confirming my statement, then he turns to me with a "you fucker" look. I just spotted his stripes, and he knows it.

We settle in, driving through Guerrero's dirt roads. It would be a waste of time to ask where we are going. This town is not a hotspot for the Mexican Cartel, which makes me wonder why we are here. The citizens are all carrying pistols, like the Old West. Not too many robberies around here; they just get dead.

This driver is good. I counted four heat runs. He's making sure we don't have a tail or any air surveillance. The German probably has mercs on rooftops with high-end glass, looking for drones, planes, or UFOs. The heat runs are done in circles, making it easier to spot any aircraft at high altitudes.

Rodeo Boy's phone rings. After two seconds, he tells the driver, "Estamos bien, Joe."

Rodeo Boy just crumbed the play. The driver stiffens up and wrings the steering wheel. He is pissed Rodeo Boy used his name. He looks at me, and I'm just looking out the window, ignoring the fuckup. The ass-kicking this merc, "Joe," is going to give that kid…good thing the kid is wearing a red shirt to camouflage the blood.

We pull up to a small house on the west side of town with four Suburbans parked outside. Two sentries stand by the driveway, packing AK-47s. We check in, get waved in, and pull up to the front of the house. Joe is good—he's using the vehicle as a barrier between the house and everything else.

Four mercs appear out of thin air. They walk up to my door and stop. Joe gives them a nod, giving them clearance to pull me out. The door swings open and down I go. A full pat-down, not only for weapons, but recording, bugs, and tracking devices. I'm stripped down to my bare ass, and they go through every piece of my clothes. As I stand there wearing nothing but a smile, Joe gets a small tool out of his pocket and begins to unscrew my knives, checking for tracking devices. These guys are as good as they come, not missing a thing.

"Joe, I want those blades put back right. I'm no hey boy, you got me?"

Joe smiles and gives me a nod, knowing the attachment people like us have to our edge weapons. I trust he will do the right thing.

I'm allowed to dress, but not before they've marveled over my Vince sneakers. After I get put back together, they sandwich me and we walk in sync like a high school fucking marching band to the main house to meet the German.

As we walk into the house, four more mercs are waiting and they give me a half-assed pat down. While they are doing this, I canvass the room for exits, weapons, pictures of people I can use as conversation. Good to know there is no plastic on the floor—not getting hit today.

About ten yards away, I can see the German walking toward me. He is wearing a beautiful, shiny, silver suit that's been tailor made by who knows who. In his left hand, he is carrying a gold and green glass tumbler half-full of some expensive whisky. The killer of hundreds gracefully turns and gestures for me to sit in a rusty, piece-of-shit, aluminum and vinyl chair, while his boys carry over a red, velvet chair for his majesty.

"Toño, you have been a very good boy, I must say," he starts with that German accent. "You must be a little worried why I have gone to all this trouble just to meet with you, yes?"

I learned from my tio the less you say, the better. I just look into his cold, blue eyes and give him a half-nod.

He looks at the four mercs looming over me and says in Spanish, "Bueno, pues relajesen, muchachos."

The four mercs move an earshot away, but you better know they're on alert for any movements. The German looks away in a pensive manner and says, "There is a little thing we will require you and your patriots to do for us, yes."

I don't take this statement as a question, so I continue to sit in this piece-of-shit chair, acting like I own it. I know everything I do in front of the German will be noticed. It is not a mistake he sat me in this chair. As uncomfortable as I am, I sit back, cross my legs—to show off my socks and sneakers—and hold a half-smile to confuse the bastard. The game is afoot.

"You will take a locked suitcase to Fort Worth, Texas. Upon arrival, you will set up shop and check out the lay of the land. You will secure the suitcase in a safe location. Then, you will meet with our comrades in Rock Island, yes? You will then work out a time and place to deliver said case to El Teco. Yes, he's the same chap you insulted during the plane drop you made."

This German is well informed on all our movements and actions. Fucking scary.

"After the delivery, you will take into possession a package and return it to me personally. Is all this clear, or must you write it down?" The German says this as he leans toward me with a cold, dead look on his face. I stare back for a moment before giving him a short nod for the second time.

I guess he's had enough of my silent nodding, because he stands up and turns away from me with his hands behind his back. He whispers in a deep, dark voice, "You will answer me with a yes, you understand, or I will open your throat to check if you have vocal cords."

I found a chink in his armor. I got to the un-gettable. I got to the German. I say with a low, monotone voice, "We shall follow your directions to the letter, comrade."

"Testy, are we? Do I make you nervous?"

What to say? Usually, I would smart off with a "not as much as this chair," or "not from a little man like you, Boy Jorge." But that would be the end of me. No, I will play his game to the end and not be stupid. "Sir, I respect you and fear you. If I don't do your bidding, well, we know what the consequences will be."

The German is surprised by my response. He turns and gives me a bewildered look. "You are more than what is presented today. I have said it before—you are one to keep an ever-watchful eye on, comrade. The action you did with El Commandante's daughter was well documented in your skills box. But, beware, this job is more than a task. These Rock Island Boys are not to be trifled with. Your remarks to El Teco were brought up and made some none too happy. These city cowboys are battle-tested and, in the blink of an eye, will dismember you. Treat them like Raptors."

How the hell did he find out I called them that? This guy probably knows my blood type.

"Toño, you said 'we'?"

Here is where I have to dance the two-step. "My boys for cover and muscle."

"Ah, an ever-watchful eye for the assault." The German has a lot of military training, but for which side did he work for before he started working as a merc for the highest bidder?

"I only have one question, sir. When and where do I make the pickup of the suitcase, and what is in the suitcase?"

"What is in the suitcase is not of your concern, yes."

"No, sir, just details—will the contents break, will it blow up if not handled properly, can it get wet?"

"I see. Yes, well, I will tell you what is "the contents of the case"—money. And before you ask me what you shall be bringing back, let's just say it's the size of a shoebox. I will warn you now not to open the suitcase, for I will know."

He didn't have to say it—it's part of the job description to never look in the case. If you do, life will be bleak.

"You will meet a boat at the Oso Blanco dock at nine tonight."

This German is scaring the shit out of me. No emotion in his words or body language, just pure evil in an expensive suit. At a look, the four horsemen close in and stand me up. You never stand up without being told.

The German turns away, staring at the bare territory behind the house.

Off I go, sandwiched all the way to the Suburban. The driver has pointed it toward the street. I sit quietly in the passenger seat, trying to be as cool as possible. One of the horsemen takes the backseat behind the driver. I give Joe a "where is red shirt boy" look. Joe just shrugs his shoulder. I return the gesture.

The drive back was shorter. Only three heat runs and I'm back at my truck. We stop, and I don't bolt like I want to, but just sit and wait. Joe looks at me. I look at him.

Joe catches himself, pulls my blades from his cargo pocket, and reluctantly hands me my knives. He finally says, "I heard what you did in South Padre Island—that turn and poke on one of our boys. Don't get froggy with me, because it won't be that easy."

I pick up an accent from Joe, but I just can't place it.

"Joe, you of all people should know there is no money in that action." I bail out of the truck, back up four steps, and wait for the mercs to leave.

That Joe is a true professional. He backs out, never taking his eyes off me. I'll see him again.

Standing on the dirt road outside Pelotas pool hall in Guerrero, Mexico is not what I call pleasant. I inspect my truck to make sure nothing got attached, like a tracker or car bomb. I'm not worried about the German, but the rival drug runners might think I am poaching on their turf. Life is dangerous on the border however you slice it.

I'm back on the road to Zapata with a lot of problems in my path and not one answer. The German must know that I would figure out this drop and roll with a meet and greet is a death drop. It reminds me of that scene in *Scarface* where the Colombians chainsaw the Corpitos-born actor in the bathtub. I don't want to be playing catch-up with the German.

Hold on—I'm a river rat trained by the best villain in Texas, my tio. I have made many a move for these guys and never had the top man give me explicit orders on a piece of work. Why now? This is all fucked up, a simple drop and roll with a meet and greet in the middle. And to screw it up even more, I have to do the job with that Rock Island Funky Town piece of work El Teco—and in his backyard? That puto is going to want to have some words with this Texican. El Teco's tats don't make him hard; they just make it easier to pick him out of a lineup. Just ask Jay, my pachuco backup. He's been picked out of many a lineup, even when he didn't do it, which is not too often.

It's time to pull out the toolbox and think about what and who we will need to pull this job off and still live to turn the tables on whoever is trying to play us.

Why the hell did the German tell me what was in the case? He could be lying about the money. The German keeps you off balance so he can push you over at any time.

These are the times I wish my tio hadn't tried to set me up with the cartel and have me killed. He would have already known what was up before the sit with the German. My tio was in the smugglers' racket for twenty years before he pulled his Houdini, leaving us top dogs on the porch. But he knew that would happen. Well, what I don't have in years, I have in smarts. The Mexican Cartel using their main enforcer to send us to get slaughtered. Or maybe it will be cakewalk. Right!

BORDER COPS ARE ALL THE SAME

The drive to the Mexican checkpoint is short but treacherous. They always shake me down for some coin. Entering Mexico is much easier than leaving, trust me. I see two short federales. Their eyes widen and they start to smile upon my approach. They see my King Ranch truck and know I have money they want to relieve me of. I pull up and it starts.

"Que bonita troca, me la vendes," one says with a big smile.

Knowing I'm clean, I decide to fuck with these low-level hustlers with badges.

I step out of the truck and motion to them. "La quieren, el dueno es El Tony de reinosa, tomanla." Now, El Tony is a serious cartel boss that handles all the movement in Reynosa, Mexico across the border from Brownsville, Texas.

They must know what's who because they take three steps back and both wave me through all polite, as if to say they are very sorry.

Funny thing is, I don't even know El Tony.

Driving over the bridge brings back memories of when we crossed a ton of shit right under it. Customs never thought of patrolling under their office. Those were creative days, and we made money, baby. I pull up to the US side of the bridge, which is a cakewalk when you're clean.

"Good afternoon, sir, are you an American citizen?" this young customs agent asks in this authoritative tone.

Remembering the less you say the better, I answer, "Yes."

"Are you bringing anything into my country?"

"No."

"Not one thing? Nothing? Bullshit, what are you bringing back?" This Iowa farmer boy just out of the academy is getting red-faced. "Pull that piece of shit over for inspection."

I look at the customs office and I see Ito through the blinds, laughing his ass off. Pinche Ito set me up with this newbie. As this new customs agent begins to rip through my truck, I can hear the rest of the agents in the office laughing, so I join in. It was fucking funny.

After thirty minutes, Ito finally comes out and pats the newbie agent on his back and says, "Joe, you done good, but he's clean. Go inside before you fry out here."

"Pinche Ito, no vales verga," I have to say with half a smile.

"I told you about ripping your truck apart when you came back through."

"I know, but I thought you were just putting me on."

"We have to break in the new guys. It was just your turn, Toño."

"I'm going to get you back, Ito. I don't know how, but I'm going to get you back, puto." I hop in my truck and drive off with half a smile.

There is fuckery afoot on this travel to Fort Worth. First things first; I need to get my crew up and running. I will need my boys, Rigo, Paco, and Pachuco Jay, if he isn't in jail. We will also need a ringer, a local or two, for this move. The ringer has to be somebody that can walk in anywhere and blend in. The best. My tio used someone several years ago who would be perfect. She is only known as Chiquita. She got her name from an old movie with Lee Marvin and Burt Lancaster. Chiquita is as tough as any man; she can kiss you or kill you with the same enthusiasm. Chiquita lives in the South San section in San Antonio. She's about 5'3", with a solid frame, great ass, and long, black hair. One story goes she was tasked to go into the Menger Hotel bar and keep an eye on a guy that an S.A. crew wanted to hit. The target began to hit on her, being vulgar and insulting. The old Menger bar has an upstairs that's very quiet because they don't have waiters, just bartenders, so not many patrons drink up there. Chiquita cornered this guy up there and gutted him from his buckle to this throat. He must have really pissed her off because she got personal. They say they didn't find the guy till closing time. Half his guts were on the floor. She is as tough as they come. I'll reach out to her for our ringer.

Locals who know the landscape might be a bit riskier; we don't want word to get back to the Rock Island Boys and El Teco about our moves. My last trip to Fort Worth, I met two dudes, Hunter and Paesan, that helped us with a drop. These two guys are funnier than shit, and they know the town and all the villains. They also run all the good gambling places in the metroplex. They're the movers and shakers in Funky Town, and they sure can party. My tio trusted them even though they drink vodka like it's going out of style. I'll have to keep them away from Pachuco Jay.

They're both in their late forties. Hunter looks like a duplicate of Telly Savalas and could talk himself out of hell and walk out with a pocketful of pesos while doing it.

The story goes Hunter had one of his gambling houses raided. All his clients were arrested and bused to the Tarrant County Jail. This fucking Hunter gets a bus and waits for the gamblers at the jail.

He and Paesan are wearing dark suits when they flash a badge to the cops that are transporting the prisoners. "The FBI is taking over this case. We are going to file this federally and go for the big fish."

Well, the cops, not wanting to book in twenty-five prisoners, load them in the bus and they drive off. The Vice detectives arrive hours later to the jail—after confiscating all the gambling tables and slot machines—asking where the prisoners are locked up. The transport cops just said the Feds took them. By then, everyone was in the wind. They were so embarrassed they never filed the case.

The balls on these two guys drag when they walk. I swear, you can't make this shit up. I dare you to even try.

Paesan is from Little Italy in NYC and learned from the best number runners. His specialty is collection of outstanding debt. He's 5'10", 175 pounds of pretty boy. Don't let his size fool you—you don't want to get in a scrape with this guy. I would hate to see him and Rigo go toe to toe.

Paesan was once sent to collect on a $20,000 debt a rich cowboy owed from a bad day on the tables. This cowboy's favorite hangout was the Del Frisco's restaurant. He was always there with his running buddies. Paesan, being from NYC, is a crafty sort, so he watches and waits until the cowboy is good and liquored up. He just sits patiently at the bar. When the mark goes to the bathroom to water the trough, Paesan follows him at a safe pace. As the cowboy is in mid-stream, Paesan goes into the stall, takes the toilet cover in hand, walks up behind the cowboy, and smashes it over his head, dropping him like a sack of taters. Paesan takes his wallet and removes the cash for himself, along with a black American Express. Paesan walks out like he owns the restaurant.

Within twenty minutes, he'd charged $40,000 on the card, the Vig baby. They say that to this day the cowboy can't speak right. Pay your debts and this shit won't happen, as they also say.

These guys can be trusted on this type of job. I'll reach out to them and Chiquita to tie a knot on this crew. Now, all I have to do is get my boys on board. That's easier said than done.

THE CREW

Time to get my crew together for a powwow at my house, I better load up with beer or they might not come.

As I drive back on Hwy. 83, I can see the river just across to my left. Between the river and me is nothing but cactus, mesquite trees, and cattle trying to find any shade they can. Damn, it's 101 degrees today, punishing every living thing.

As I drive by Lopeno, a spot of a town with 100 folks, I'm glad I don't live out here in the sticks. Several miles down, I get to a community called El Congo and, off at the distance, I see an old friend, Chevo, out in the middle of the cactuses, "chamuscando."

Now, chamuscando is not for the weak of heart. What you do is get yourself a propane tank and rig a hose to a hollow, metal pipe with a metal cover around the end of it. You strap the tank over your shoulder, open the propane, and light it up. The flame width is controlled by how much propane you let out of the tank. Once the flame is where you want it, you start burning the cactus. When it's 101 degrees outside, with this flame, it's up to 125 degrees, and shouldering this heavy tank is a bitch. Ranchers burn cactus when they can't afford feed for the cattle. It's a hard life in South Texas, but we make it work.

I honk at Chevo, but propane burning makes a loud whoosh that drowns out everything. I'd rather deal with the wolves than burn cactus any day.

How am I going to pass off this job to my crew as business as usual? They are going to smell fresh-cut cow horn. If you have never smelled the stench of fresh-cut cattle horns, let me tell you; it's worse than anything you can possibly think of. Years back, before all you had to do was give cattle a shot and their horns would fall off, you had to cut them like tree limbs. You would pin them in what's called a cattle shoot and cut the horns one by one. I get sick just thinking of the smell.

I make the final turn toward my Hacienda and the dogs are quiet—too quiet. Something's not right, so I stop around the bend, lower my windows, and sit and listen. I hear nothing but the wind; it's chilling.

Until, suddenly, "Toño, you worry too much, puto!"

It's Pachuco Jay with that pinche cholo song in his voice. I have to say I am relieved. I laugh as I start up my truck and drive the rest of the way in. These guys knew if they kept the dogs quiet, I would drop to survival mode. Never go to them; make them come to you, and you will always have an edge.

I'm going to have to change my tactics. I've become predictable, like a boxer who steps with his jab. All they have to do is time the step, and down you go.

I pull up and see the three amigos sitting on my porch. Jay always takes the right side. He always has an exit route everywhere he goes. You will never catch him in the middle of a crowd. He's spent too many years in prison to expose his six to shanks, sucker punches, or yard beatdowns. The two brothers, Paco and Rigo, are just sitting and smiling. They must be up to something.

Jay pops up, and I notice he's wearing new duds and shoes. Damn! He's wearing shiny, black, pointy Stacy Adam shoes with an extra half-sole that lifts his toes up an inch. He's showing off baby-blue socks that match his baby-blue slacks and a white wife beater. Jay is flying his gang tats—riatas and other prison ink that he's very touchy about. He walks up with that pachuco lean, shoulders back, almost falling backward.

"Beer, joto."

I just point to the back of my truck, where I have an ice chest full. One of Jay's rays of sunshine will always be beer—well, free beer.

As Jay blows by me, I fix my attention on the two brothers. They are still smiling, not moving or saying a word. I stop dead in my tracks. "What, my zipper down?"

Paco stands. "What did you do now, Toño? I knew it was going to happen sooner or later. I told you they were going to make a play for us."

"Mira, holmes, I just asked you guys to meet me here at the house. I didn't say anything about anything."

Paco, with those smiling eyes, says, "Toño, we know you went to Guerrero. And why would you go to Guerrero? Come on, dude, we're not stupid."

As I begin to rip into Paco, I turn and see three beer cans by my truck and, standing in the bed, Jay is chugging his fourth.

I yell, "Jay, get the ice chest down so we all can have a beer, Bad Santa."

"Fuck you, Toño, I'm thirsty."

"Get over here, boy. Here is the deal—it's a drop and roll with a meet and greet in the middle."

To that, I receive dead silence.

DROP AND ROLL

"Drop and roll with a meet and greet in the middle?"

"You got that right, Rigo. Would be pretty simple if I hadn't been given the job directly from the German.

Now Rigo stands. "You met the German today in Guerrero? What was he wearing?"

"Man, he was wearing a killer suit. It was handmade with the matching square and a cravat with a mid-break on the coat collar."

"I can't believe you guys are talking about clothes. Fuck his suit, what did he want?"

I glare at Paco, as I rarely have to with this soldier. Silence fills the air. Paco drops his shoulders and head a couple inches.

"Paco, take a step back and really think about where you are and who you are talking to. We are alive and running the big show because of my moves." My voice always sounds like a lifetime smoker after his third pack of Camel unfiltereds when I'm pissed. I square off, noticing Rigo with a side-glance. Is this the day Paco decides to be alpha of the pack? I feel Jay shadow my right side with that calm, calculating walk you can't mistake for anything else but trouble brewing. Paco looks at me and knows we're like brothers, but right now, it's submit, cut, and run, or we pull our quetes and start gouging away, western style.

As we stand on the porch like statues, Paco finally sticks his hands in his pockets and asks, "What papos was the German wearing?"

Rigo sits down and crosses his legs with a sigh of relief.

I look back at Jay and use the same line the German used on his mercs to stand down: "Bueno, pues relajate, hombre."

Jay drops the ice chest between us and gives Paco that pachuco look only he can get away with.

As Jay reaches for the ice chest and another beer, I step on the lid, so my crew knows I'm serious and none-too-happy with their behavior.

The German—the fucking German paged me up to Guerrero like a fucking lapdog, surrounded by a bunch of his mercs. I didn't know if I would make it back. Then I come back to my crew, which I am protecting and stuffing feria in their pockets, and this is how they greet me? "If any of you motherfuckers want the reigns of this outfit and want to deal with this whole mess of catfish, now is the time to make your move." I never yell, but my voice jumps a notch with every word.

All three raised their hands like they were giving up to a SWAT team. "No, it's yours, were cool."

"I don't ever want to talk about this again, comprenden?" I must have sold my position because all I got was heads down in submission and a bunch of okays.

This airing out between a crew is inevitable; it comes with a group of hard men living a hard life. My tio told me to expect this kind of shit every two to three years.

He told me a story. Three years ago, he had a bit of a mutiny from the guy that El Machete replaced. My tio had a meet with all his executives at El Mesquite Ranch. Let's just say I would never eat on the table at that ranch. Some things you just can't un-see, and this was one of them. It involved my tio's set of machetes, each with a different weight and length for specific jobs and specialty cuts. When the sun came up, he used these machetes again on the guy, because he didn't have the eyesight he used to pull off the precision he was going for in the dark. He likes to see his handiwork and the looks on his people's faces as he's carving. What's the use of doing a Jason if you don't have a crowd?

I take my boot off the ice chest and Paco hands me a beer with the only apologetic look I've ever seen from him. I nod. Now, it's time to get back on task.

"Back to work. The cartel wants us to deliver a package to El Teco in Fort Worth. Then, we are to bounce back with a package. I'm, then, supposed to deliver the package to the German personally—hopefully in Guerrero, but I wasn't told. The German wants us to set up shop in Fort Worth for a day or two before we do the drop. I'm thinking El Teco is tightly holding this package for now. I'm thinking when we ask for the package, the brouhaha will start—and draw, pop, and drop will be the flavor of the day."

"Wait a minute, I don't understand. We take a package, give it to tattoo boy and his crew?"

"The Rock Island Boys, Jay."

"Great. Then, he's supposed to hand us the German's package and we bounce. But, you're saying there is going to be a problem?"

"Think about it. This is my tio's teaching on how the cartel works. They're cheap when they want competition or need problem crews gone. They usually set up a play to have them take each other out. The meet with El Teco keeps bothering me. Why was that Fort Worth boy so pissed at us on our meet and drop by the plane? A visitor in the middle of a ranch in our backyard, facing three locals loaded for bear. I don't care how bad or seasoned in our business you are, you usually have your hat in your hand. That didn't make sense until now."

"I get it—he feeds El Teco a bunch of shit about us, and the Rock Island Boy gets all lathered up and prepares a welcoming gangster party for us."

"Not bad, Rigo."

"Fuck you, Toño, I'm on top of it. So, now what do we do?"

"Well, boys, whatever I or we come up with, I need to know you guys are ready to jump in the ring and put in the work."

Rigo, in true fashion, jumps up. "Let's kill the fucking German. We can take him."

"I have twenty reasons why we can't take that bull down. So, I'll just ask one thing—who are his employers?"

Rigo gets this blank stare and says, "Well, okay, I'm in."

I turn to see where my Pachuco Jay is on this hunt. He stares at his beer for several seconds, until he knocks it down in one gulp, gives a burp, and says, "I'm out, Toño. I can see they want us gone, and I'm too long in the tooth to scrap it out anymore. I'm going back to my chante in Laredo to watch novelas and live out my life in peace and quiet."

Jay has spent most of his life in prison. He has been stabbed, cut, shot, spit and shit on, dragged, and called everything but a white man. A man like Jay has lived by the feud all his life. Every one of us only has so many rodeos before we give out. There is always an end to the road we travel. Jay has earned his place in the sun.

I face Jay, as do Paco and Rigo. With as much respect as we can muster, we all start laughing and shoving Jay around, until he starts laughing.

"I'm serious, I'm not going," Jay stammers with a smirk.

I stop laughing and advise Jay if we work out this fiasco, we might split a large chunk of coin between us.

"How much?"

"Well, I will know later, but I'm thinking enough for you to retire in Monterrey."

"I'm in!" Jay yells.

Paco follows suit with a big smile.

All I have to do is figure out how to work out a plan to drop and roll with a meet and greet without getting any of us killed—and how to keep the German's money. Easy as pie!

PREPARING FOR THE ROLL

After a long night of drinking with my bottomless crew, I feel like I've aged ten years. I wake up with one boot on, I'm missing my belt, and my shirt is on inside out. You know, I'm not even going to ask. It was a big party last night, and the best thing of all was that everybody left. It's always nice not having to wake a bunch of drunks and get them to leave when you have a Charlie Harper hangover. I was always told: "If you're man enough to stay out late, you better be man enough to get up early to work."

Two aspirin chased with a hot beer and I'm off for my workout to sweat the night out. Start with 100 push-ups, 150 sit-ups, and pull-ups till failure. No run today, I'm way past the idea of three miles in this heat. It's 9:00 a.m. and already ninety-five degrees and humid as hell. It's great for a sweat, but I would die today.

After my maintenance workout and a quick shower, time to visit the kitchen. My maid has made coffee the old way, with some calabaza shavings. She boils water in this old tub, dumps the coffee grounds into the hot water, and sweetens it with the sugar calabaza candy. I grab my favorite blue ceramic coffee cup with a sunflower on the side—you know, that one cup that fits your hand just right. I grab the strainer, place it over my cup, and pour the black tar. It's my black gold baby, devil's blood.

Sitting alone in my kitchen and drinking sludge has always been my favorite time of day. Reflection, denial, and apologies fill my mind. Today, my mind is sharpening like a knife on an Arkansas stone. I have to call San Antonio to find Chiquita. Then, the two Fort Worth locals for housing, security, and intelligence gathering.

Six hours, eight cups of coffee, and four leftover chorizo tacos later, I'm almost done. Not "stick a fork in me" done, but I might have my ringer and locals up and running. Chiquita has vanished for another recent mistake. The story goes she clipped a guy when she was doing a pick and roll on the visitors at the Alamo. It's an old setup—you know, a bar, a girl, back to the room, then you get rolled. Simple, if you do it right.

Well, I was told her partner was drunk and busted in early before her mark got undressed. The mark reached for a hideaway belly gun. Chiquita stabbed him in the throat and bled him out right there in Room 308. The mark was related to somebody that makes things run smooth for certain people in San Antonio. Three days later, Chiquita fell off the face of the earth. What's the old saying? "You can have all the 'attaboys,' but one 'aw shit' and you're fucked."

Good thing Freddy the Saint is available after a short vacation in prison. Freddy is a bigshot in the San Antonio underworld. He is not a saint; he got the nickname from back in the day when he was an altar boy, but don't bring that up. Freddy stands 6'2", 235 pounds, has light eyes and long, black hair. He kind of looks like Tom Cruise in the face and has a very calm exterior—just don't push him. He and Chiquita worked together for years. If she's alive, he can find her.

The two locals, Hunter and Paesan, had been on an all-night affair and were having breakfast at the Paris Café. If you want the best breakfast in Fort Worth, go to the Paris. It's old school, been there forever. Hunter answers the phone and, within seconds, has me tell him how we did the South Texas drag and all about my uncle's Houdini move. After a minute of catching him up, I run down the piece of work we're planning in their town. I expected his next question.

"Who is the meet and greet with?" After a few choice words and advisements attached to the Rock Island Boys, Hunter explains that El Teco is the worst of the bunch. "This crazy cat does things in broad daylight in the middle of the street—in his barrio of course." Hunter thinks he's protected because his brother was a councilman for the city. He passes the phone to Paesan.

"Yo, Toño, how's it hanging?"

"Paesan, you mamaluke, you still alive and kicking?"

"Yeah, yeah. Hey, you making a play on the Rock Island Boys?"

"I have a drop and roll with a meet and greet in the middle, that's it. It just happens to be in your town with the worst guys. Oh, and I have to return a package and place it at the feet of the one and only German."

"Okay, why didn't ya just say so, you motherfucker. What are you, stugats?"

"I have no idea what that means, Paesan, but remember, you guys are on our side. You work contract jobs for us, and I really need you."

"Hey, I know who you are and what weight comes with it. We are just wanting to know what sauce to use for the goose."

"Set me up two rooms, different places. Mine with an exit to move around, the other, I don't want to know where."

"You got it, forget about it."

"That's better. I have my boys and hopefully my ringer moving up to Funky Town today. So, my question is, after we make some moves and pick a pocket or two, you guys want a percentage or flat rate?"

Paesan mutes the phone to consult with Hunter. He gets back on and says, "We have no idea how you're making coin on this, so it will be flat rate, Toño."

"Ten grand each is the rate, boys." Hunter, knowing he has me on the dangle, grabs the phone. "Ten grand an eye, Toño. We will get your digs and anything else you need."

"All right, ten grand an eye, you thief. We will be needing short, medium, and long hardware as soon as we get to the digs. Have the Farrier meet us with all his dry goods, okay?"

"You will have him at the digs with all his dry goods. I leave him in the dark, because that guy can't keep his mouth shut."

"Hey, Hunter, is that towheaded Kentucky Windage shooter still around?"

"Rick the Stick! That boy can shoot that long rifle, Toño. Remember what he did in Stop Six the last time you boys came up?"

"Yeah, see if you can reach out to him and put him on retainer before the Rock Island Boys do. And find out all about El Teco's brother."

"Okay, but if you're going to need me and Paesan to help bake the pie, we want a slice above the flat rate."

"No worries. I'll text you when we are close. And boys, stay away from the vodka. I need you clear-eyed."

"Fuck you, we are professionals, Toño. The party never ends, you river rat."

These locals know they will be getting in the middle of the dance between the cartel and Rock Island. They must be seeing an upside to jump in.

"One more thing, Hunter. Can you get Snow White to poke around the outskirts of Rock Island and see what they're up to?"

"I just saw her last night. Tough as nails and twice as pretty. I'll get her on the hunt as soon as I finish my fucking breakfast. Bye."

Snow White is the yin to Chiquita's yang. Her dad was in the Air Force and brought her to the Laredo base from wherever they were from—Denmark, Finland, Minnesota, someplace like that. Her dad was never home and left Snow White unsupervised in Laredo. Well, she hooked up with the bad element and by the age of sixteen, she became la gringa with Spanish talk. She speaks better Tex-Mex than most locals. She stands 5'7", which is tall for a woman in these parts, and she's all muscle. The girl lives in the gym with blonde hair and blue eyes that just cut right through you.

Don't let her looks fool you. She befriended a famous boxing trainer, Mickey Demos out of Miami, while he was in Laredo training a featherweight. Mickey took Snow White under his wing and trained her as a no-shit boxer. It is said she can hit you with so many lefts you'll beg her for a right. She can walk into any shithole in the South Texas Valley and have the hardest dude eating out of her hand.

Now, where the hell is Chiquita?

10

THE BOUNCE

W hat would my tio do with this mess that's sitting in front of me? I can't think this simple job is not full of deathtraps. It spells trouble from here to Crystal City. I finally get the call I was waiting for from Freddy the Saint.

A quick story about Freddy—this guy doesn't drink, smoke, or cuss, but a better corner man you can't find. Freddy is just crazy without reason. I was at a party at his place years back. The cops came bitching about the noise. These two young officers walked in to a passel of villains. Freddy doesn't have an ounce of fat on him—solid as a rock. Well, Freddy picked up one of the cops, pressed him over his head, and threw him off the second-story balcony. As you might think, it killed the party. The other cop ran downstairs to find his partner, who never made it to the ground. The flying cop was dangling from a mesquite tree. No blood, no foul. The cops didn't see it that way. Freddy was on the dash and slept in a tree all night. Ironic.

Yes, he's crazy, but what a corner man. I'm going to put him on retainer for this jump.

"Where is she, Freddy?"

"Why should I tell you? I've been asked hard by those putos looking for her."

"How bad do they want her?"

"Not bad enough to kill me. They only sent two guys to press me."

"Two guys? You put them in the meat wagon?"

"Good to have a reputation, Toño. They pressed for a while, then I had enough and just stood up. All they said was, 'Okay, okay, so you don't know where Chiquita is,' and they left. These guys aren't pros. More like pissed-off family shit."

"Freddy, I might need you on this hunt as an end-around, not a pusher up front."

"I'm free. Who's the mark?"

"Rock Island, a guy named El Teco."

"Toño, I have to tell you—that guy, I know him. It's not that he's crazy, but he has this thing about respect, honor, and he will die and sacrifice his whole crew over it and they follow him like Imhotep. Blind obedience. He does have a weakness—his brother. I met him when I was collecting, which is my thing now. Roberto the Shark was a city councilman bigshot in Funky Town. Some say he was in line for mayor. Roberto had to give up his council seat and politics because of what El Teco was bleeding on his precinct's streets. Get this, Roberto is now a bigtime card player. Not a good one—hence, I met him to collect twenty grand on a bad night with the Bosnians. And you know them."

"Yeah, I know those lopovs. They're heavy in Laredo because they're all truck drivers. They run most of the whores now."

"Well, I was supposed to meet Roberto to collect the twenty grand at a place called the Mercury Chophouse. Why do they think if it's a nice place, you won't smash their head into the table? The owner, Zack, walked me to the back table to meet Roberto. I walked into El Teco and his crew sitting with Roberto, doing a Sinatra. You know I don't like to talk when I'm working, so I just wave to the glass plate window and there sits Chiquita with two MAC-10 submachine guns, smiling. Roberto sits up and waves El Teco back.

"Roberto says with a nervous tone, 'Now, Freddy, I know I owe twenty large. I can give you ten now. Can I get you the rest next week?' Roberto was smart enough to yank his brother's chain. So, we now know El Teco bows to his brother, and that's useful. I took his ten grand and his BMW as collateral. Chiquita would have peppered that room up and they knew it. Roberto is El Teco's weak spot."

"Fuck, Freddy, for a guy that doesn't talk, you sure are spilling at the mouth."

"Fuck you, Toño. Be nice or I won't tell you where Chiquita is. She said she needs to get out of San Antonio, at least until the heat is off. She's yours. Pick her up on your way up to Funky Town. Text me when you're in Sananto, and I'll tell you where."

"Tell her it's a two-day gig, no hardware needed, but bring her blades. I have the Farrier coming to fit us with a toolbox. Freddy, you slide in behind. We will have eyes on us, so watch our back. I'm going to need intel on who is watching us, what they are driving, and what hardware they are packing. I will match your rate, and maybe sweeten the pot if it all rolls our way."

"Toño, you watch that Teco. He cheats. He has a habit of carrying a Northern Arms .22 caliber derringer in his right pocket. He has more than one pair of pants with holes, if you know what I mean."

Yeah, a pocket shooter, great! As I hang up, I catch myself straying away from the path of what is really in play. I might be wrong about the cartel pairing us for a gladiator fight. If these pinche putos had the balls, they would just cut us down. But they need us smugglers. Without us, who will step in with the connections and talent to move the flavor of the month? They would have to freelance and contract the jobs to whoever can handle the work. Not a real good place to be when the bosses expect money not mistakes. Not even the German is immune to a hit. I wouldn't advise it, but it could happen.

The simpler the job, the harder it is. I have a couple hours before I pick up the suitcase by the Oso Blanco boat ramp. I'll get Paco to cover me with his deer slayer, just in case something goes wrong. I was told to come alone, but fuck them. This is my turf and, in this life, rules are becoming more like guidelines by their own doing. Damn! I wish my tio were around for a powwow on this game. He would have the answers I'm still looking for and know the moves to counter.

I'll figure it out, but it will take more information than what I have right now.

Time to go home to pack, shower, and write another letter to my maid, just in case I don't make it back. She always says the same thing in broken English: "Stop what you're doing, you're killing your mother." A life like mine is not pursued by choice but necessity. I've described it as walking barefoot in sand that's burning your feet. When you find shade, you jump to it, and, after a while, it's too painful to move. You're stuck, centered and left wanting with regrets.

What the hell am I babbling about? Oh, right, I love the action and money. It seems to soothe the pain of being owned like someone's racehorse.

Calling Paco is like pulling teeth. They either never answer or let the phone ring ten times. Hey, one ring, and Paco is on the hook.

"Paco, get your .308 cal. rifle. We are on a pickup in sixty minutes."

"Are we expecting trouble?"

"Nah, I'm more worried about some local seeing an opportunity to jack us. A lot of new faces around don't know us."

"Okay, I'll do the cover, but Rigo also wants to go."

"Sure, if he wants, but you guys pack for our jump right after. Call Jay and have him ready to roll. He can come to the pickup if he wants, or we can grab him up on the way. His call."

Done and done.

Now, time to pick out my duds. I'll wear my liberty boots with longhorns embroidered on the front, my dark blue Mossimo jeans, and my Ryan long-sleeved snap shirt. My belt of choice is handmade alligator with a designer buckle from Tillman's Restaurant. Fill my Brooks Brothers leather bag with utility cloth and my spare Bed/Stu lace-up boots, just in case I have to put foot to ass. (I don't want to scratch up my Liberties.)

As I walk out to my truck, I take a moment to appreciate all that I have. A cool chante. I could never afford it if I were a square citizen. I have to get my mind right on this task. I load my Glocks in my hidden cutout compartment on my driver-side door and throw my bag in the bed. We are going to need all the room—five hitters on the roll with a seven-hour stretch to Funky Town.

But first, the lift on the river.

THE LIFT

I t's pinche hot out here, as always. The ground has that glare coming off it. I have seen tires melt in this shit before. Nombre, it is a hard land for hard people. If you're weak in South Texas, you will live a miserable life. It suffers no fools. As I drive off from my hacienda, it always hits me—will this be the last time my eyes capture the beauty of this piece of land?

Fuck it. With what we are about to do, I just can't care about anything. We need to go into the job with a blank slate and sharp eyes, cutting right into whatever crosses our path, rock hard and committed. Trying to stop a villain is dangerous if you're not prepared to lance that boil.

Driving out to my hometown, I can see why people are leaving. They're looking for opportunities and don't want to brush shoulders with true villains like me and my crew. Now that my tio is in the wind, we are the ones they whisper about when we walk by. That's okay; I'd still rather be feared or hated than ignored.

I stop at Chapa's gas station for some petrol and an earful from Mr. Chapa about how the Zapata Hawks football team sucks this year. Just as I pull up to the pump, it starts.

"Toño, come here, did you hear what that pinche coach did? He changed quarterbacks."

"No way, Mr. Chapa. You better go straighten that baboso out!"

"Don't think I won't. They just don't make players like you anymore. Why didn't you go play college football, Toño?"

I pause and give him a "you're kidding, right?" look. He knows the road I was shoved down when my pop died. Mr. Chapa and my dad were good friends and Lions Club brothers, and that's a big deal here in Zapata. Mr. Chapa gets this sad look on his face and turns away.

"Another life, maybe, Mr. Chapa. Con respeto."

Mr. Chapa just glances at me with a wave. I hope it's not a look of disgust.

Off to pick up my crew, and what a crew they are. I thought they were going to write a song about us after that South Texas drag we did in Mexico. I wonder whatever happened to that girl we kidnapped—Lorraine: UT. I bet she's giving those fucking cheerleader coaches a full can of shit. I liked her grit, and sometimes that's all you need. Along with a great ass.

The town seemed happy to get rid of my tio and that fat fuck, Machete. Replacing them like we did wasn't done without a lot of luck and strategy. I will keep that to myself, close to the vest. Stories don't need to change until the final page is turned. If the Mexican Cartel or El Commandante thought for a second that I, or my crew, knew where my tio was, they would get the pliers and torches out for a Q&A. I'll tell you right now, if I knew where he was, I would tell the German and his bosses in the Mexican Cartel. My tio would know you have to spill, or you lose. He's out there covered with a blanket of anonymity, and you can bet he is alone. You can't hide from the cartel running in pairs. No, he is small and quiet in a corner of the world, waiting to make his move, and

I know he will. All I can hope for is that I'm not in his crosshairs. He knows he crossed the line trying to have me—his own family—killed. He's probably proud of how I turned the tables on the Mexican Cartel, El Commandante, and him.

I'll bet you all the mescal in Mexico that I will cross paths with him again. How to play that one, I can't worry about; I need to stay on point.

12

THE WHITE BEAR

Driving into the Medina Addition section of Zapata always has a strange feel to it. The only way I can describe it is like when you walk by your grandfather's room and sense someone or something is in there watching you. My mom always said: "Don't be scared of the dead. It's the living you have to watch." Medina Addition has the feeling of ghosts banging around. Must be all the dead bodies buried in the fields. I turn the corner and my crew, all three of them, are standing by the road, packed and ready. I was sure I would have to be busting their asses. They must smell danger in the air.

"Load up, boys, we are on a lift."

"Toño, you sure all we need is my .308 cal. rifle?"

"Yes, Paco, I don't want be worried about La Jura profiling us on I-35 and finding pistols or Jay's grenades."

"I don't have those bombs. I sold them for a pretty penny, ese."

"I know you did. My boy Jorge said they were the best fishing bait they ever used. Jorge dropped those grenades in Falcon Lake, and that's why we had that huge fish fry at the county fair."

"Hey, I don't know anything about that, but I got four new tires for my '70 Dodge Purple People Eater and stayed drunk for five days."

"Okay, we are going to the Oso Blanco lodge for the lift. I'm meeting the boatman at the dock, not the Fisherama. Paco, I will drop you off at the boat storage and cover from the south. You will have a short 180- to 200-yard shot, but you will have to shoot over the pool.

"What if snowbirds or oil field workers are swimming in the pool?"

"Paco, that pool has been dry since Mr. Torres owned it. Rigo and Jay, you guys stay in the truck." I reach down into my driver-side door cutouts, pull my Glocks, and hand them to Rigo and Jay.

"Pinche Toño, why do you have your guns and we don't?"

"I only have two cutouts. Where you guys going to hide your pistols?"

"What about the rifle, smartass?"

"This is Texas, Rigo. They're legal to have. And being from South Texas, we are expected to have deer rifles."

"Okay, I keep forgetting you're the big noise now."

"Jay, what the fuck is bothering you? Spit it out."

"Okay, I'm going to say it. I think this is just a regular drop and roll like we have made chingos of times. If they wanted to drop us in a hole, they would just do it. Ya, I said it."

"Paco and Rigo, what do you guys think?"

"Toño, we leave the thinking up to you, but it does seem like overkill."

"Hey, you guys might be right. I might be worrying about a whole lot of nothing. But remember who taught me the game—my tio, El Maestro. Let me take you down memory lane, my compadres.

"One, we kidnapped El Commandante's daughter. Two, we outfoxed my tio. His plan was to have me stabbed by that river jumper in South Padre Island and the Mexican Cartel. Three, we faced the German and his mercs and lived. Four, my tío and El Machete pulled a Houdini and escaped the long arm of the cartel. Five, we have the powwow with that city boy El Teco at the dirt airstrip in Zapata. That meet was jacked up. I think it was a viewing by the cartel to have *them* size us up. Six, I get ordered to Guerrero and have a face to face with that scary-ass German. Man, his suit was badass. All this for just a simple drop and roll? Oh, and I forgot to tell you, the German told me what was in the case we are about to pick up."

"Bullshit, Toño! He would never do that."

"Jay, I shit you not, ese puto told me what was in the case—money."

"Holy shit, this outhouse stinks, Toño. You know I've been around, and when you lay it out like that, I catch your drift."

"Are we good, boys? I really don't want to ever go over this novela again." I must have hit the mark, because all three sat quietly. "Vatos, I'm not sure why the German called me in for the meeting. I think the way they escorted me around, he was checking me out for the big 'Adiós, motherfucker!'" It felt like he was having the last laugh on account of the drag we did in Mexico. It didn't make him look bad because he returned the cocaine my tío stole, but we outplayed the un-outplayable. "I know on the surface it looks like a regular drop and roll with a meet and greet, but Jay, this sound regular to you?"

"Dude, it reminds me of when I was in Huntsville Prison and the Riatas gang asked me to transport some hash to the Brotherhood. Simple, right? But I had to drop it off in the basement, where all the crazies do anything to survive. I'm not a stranger to setups, and this just had that feeling. The late Juan Mo Time had stolen the hash and sold it to feed his monkey. You never look at what's in the package—Rule Number One—but I knew something was up. So, I looked, and it was wet flour. If I hadn't looked, the Brotherhood would have killed me."

"What did you do, Pachuco Jay?"

"I sold the Brotherhood a line. I told them we were getting some powerful shit next week and didn't want to fuck them with the weak shit. I told them to hold on for five days and they could double their money if they step on it right."

"What did you guys do to Juan Mo Time?"

"Rigo, I started the story with the late Juan Mo Time. I went to the captain of the Riatas and asked for a sanctioned hit."

"And that's why we are going to do a lookie-loo on that suitcase, Jay. We show up with anything but money, we will be crucified like Juan Mo Time. Wise up, guys, and let's go to work."

Rigo and Jay sit quietly, and Paco trots off to set up to glass me from the south. So far, I'm doing the obvious, what all the big players would expect. I have to start thinking backwards and sideways and not be so predictable in my chess moves.

"I'm off to the boat ramp, so you guys pelan los ojos." All I get is a small nod from Jay and Rigo, and that's good enough. I start on the stroll and remember this place twenty years back. I look over to the field by the boat storage where I learned to shoot my first .410 shotgun with my old buddy, Ito the Border Patrol pain in the ass. The lake is calm. This would be a great time to fish in the Fisherama.

The Fisherama is a floating house about twenty-five yards out from the shore. You walk out on this bridge to the house and it has an outside walking porch with rails. On the inside, the center is cut out so you can sit around and drop your fishing line. Lights fixed on the water attract the minnows, and then the white bass come a' callin'. I'm still so pissed at Oilfield Wesly. To this day, I won't talk to him.

We were fishing at the Fisherama with Mike the boatman and Oilfield Wesley; we call him that because he's a chainman in the oilfield rigs. We were fishing with two jig lures and catching two white bass at a time. We were even catching four-pound black bass, which is rare at the Rama. We must have caught forty to fifty fish. It was the best fishing day I had ever had and, I must confess, I have used dynamite before. Well, we were finishing around 3:00 a.m. when Oilfield Wesley caught the last fish. Then, he slid his fish on the trout line and let the line with all the fish slide out of his hand and sink to the bottom of the lake. I'm getting mad just thinking about it. I still won't talk to pinche Wesley. It could have been an epic fish fry, but no. We saw that sink with our fish.

I'm scanning everything around me and it's all copacetic. I walk out to the end of the dock by the fish-cleaning table that we didn't get to use because of Oilfield Wesley. It didn't smell too bad, because fishing has sucked since the water level dropped to record lows. Off in the distance, I see a seventeen-foot, red, fiberglass Skeeter boat slowly moving toward the ramp. I do what I'm supposed to do—hold my hands out, lift my shirt, and do the twirl. The driver is the same merc that drove me to meet the German in Guerrero Mexico, Joe. We lock eyes and nod. The two guys in the back take up the rest of the boat. I swear, it looks like it's going to sink.

They're holding M-16 assault rifles with double-stack magazines. The usual weapon preferred by the mercs is the MP5 submachine gun. It's smart—the M-16 is accurate up to 500 yards if you practice, and out in the open like we are today, that was a savvy move. I wonder where you find 6'6", 350- to 400-pound henchmen. One is dark-skinned with tribal tats on his face and neck. He looks Samoan and like a flunked-out pro ballplayer or a wrestler in a cheap suit. The other bookend has short, white-blond hair. He's really steroided out. You know how you can tell—your front teeth develop a gap when you're on that shit. Don't ask me how I know this useless shit, but I do.

Joe pulls up to the dock, never taking his eyes off me, and says, "You still have your edge weapons on you?"

I smile. "I never go anywhere without my Cold Steel blade."

"Place it behind you or I'll blow you to Mars."

Joe is just making a point of being a professional. No matter how big his two monsters are, they can't move in the boat. He knows they have the advantage weapon-wise, but I could do a swan dive and slash and stab before they raised one M-16.

"Okay, Joe." I step back three paces, eyes still locked on him, place my blade on the ground, walk over it three paces, and stop.

"Good boy," Joe says with an air of arrogance. He knows how the game is played. He just showed me he's the guy to watch, and I will. Joe signals the two monsters to hand over the suitcase between them.

You ever see a turtle on its back? These two fuckaroons are stuck. They're pushing and huffing, trying to stand up. The boat is slashing back and forth like a seesaw. I give Joe my best stone-cold stare and then start laughing. Joe lowers his head to hide his grin.

Shaking his head, he leans over, picks up the suitcase, and hands it to me. "You know what to do. Don't stray, or you will see me again."

I look him dead in the eyes. "And that is the last place you want to end up at, merc."

Now we are back in our place, admiring our skills. He's older, but all gristle. I can outmuscle him and even outlast him, but I would have to be ready to live with a missing eye or be content with pissing in a bag the rest of my life. Let's try to stay clear of this merc. This guy is like the beast in *Jeepers Creepers*—you just can never stop until he's down for good.

For the first time, Joe cracks a full smile and pops the boat in reverse, backing out and never taking his eyes off me. The boat gets far enough, and he flips it around, on his way back to wherever the fuck the German is lounging. I did find out one thing—that Joe is the German's number one boy.

Who is making the moves? Could this be a German move to take over the Mexican Cartel? I really think we are just pawns in a big play by somebody with a lot of clout and money to have the German do their bidding. Where the hell can I find out more about what is going on this turd hunt? If I don't, we will be collateral damage.

I wait until the low-riding Skeeter boat is out of sight before I pick up the hard, black Pelican suitcase. I bet it even floats. Next to the handle, the case has a master lock and a two-bit latch lock securing it. We didn't get the key, so we are just supposed to trust the German on the contents. It feels full, but of what? I drag my hand across my chest to relieve Paco from his task and drag the case back to my truck.

"Okay, Toño, open the shit up and let's do a lookie-loo."

"Rigo, what if the German rigged the case to blow? What if they rigged it to blow when El Teco and the Rock Island Boys open the case?"

"This is bullshit, Toño. A simple drop and roll turning into this?"

"Jay, be cool. We have Norma."

"Norma? What Norma, Toño?"

"Norma La Changa!" Paco rolls up from his trot. "What did Norma La Changa do?"

"Let's pay her a visit right fucking now."

"Toño, you know she's working at the clinic."

"Yeah, this case is hard plastic and she has access to an X-ray machine, putos. It's for broken bones and shit, but we can see if this case is rigged or see the outline of the contents."

"Orale, Toño. Just when I'm ready to doubt your ass, you come through like a government check."

"Fuck you, Jay. Don't hate, participate, mi pachuco."

We pick up and roll a big two minutes to the clinic. We pull into the back and there she is, leaning on the wall, smoking a Marlboro Light.

Norma "La Changa" was my high school savior. She's very smart, but more importantly, she shared the wealth of her knowledge. If she hadn't done the lean, allowing us to copy from her in math class, half of us would have flunked out. Shit, one time, she took my paper and all she said was, "Duni, let me do it for you. Chingado, you can't even copy right." Damn, I love me some Norma. She's a real South Texas star.

"Normita, we need a fast favor."

"Toño, que chingados quieren, you boys." Spanglish is Norma's only language, and she lets it fly. "Bueno pues, what is it you want? Last time, I almost lost my job when El Pato got shot and you guys raided the clinic."

"Yeah, Norma, sorry about that. But in our defense, he did live."

"How is that your defense, cabron?"

I just smile and show her the case.

"What? I'm not holding shit for you."

"Nombre, we need to see inside this Pelican case."

"That's it? Come on in. The nurse is not here, as usual. I have to do everything, Duni."

Duni was her nickname for me; it's a long story.

We walk into the clinic, and Norma lights up the X-ray machine.

"Put it on the table, Toño."

I lay the case on the table. We are all hovering around it like a kid does a big-ass present at Christmas. Or so I've heard.

Norma goes to move the case, and we all yell, "No!"

Norma lets go and gets that "oh, shit!" look. "What the fuck is in the case?"

"Norma, you eat with that mouth?"

"Fuck you, Rigo, I will tell your mom, cabron!"

"Normita, I was just playing."

"Andale, Toño, what the hell is in the case?"

"If I knew that, would we be here? Andale, mi changita, do the ray so we all know what's inside."

Reluctantly, Norma rays the case and brings out the results. No C4 or dynamite. All we are sure of is that we can see an outline of money—a lot of it.

"Okay, get out. If the lock on that case fucked the X-ray machine up, you putos are paying for it."

"Ay, Normita, why you gotta be so mean?"

"Mira, Rigo, I'm telling you, una ves mas. Leave or le voy a ablar a tu mother."

"Norma, a million thank yous, mi changita." Jay grabs the case, and we're off to the truck to prepare for the hop. Time to tailgate about this piece of work frying in our minds like chorizo in an iron skillet.

And now we know what is inside the case without popping locks.

"Pinche Toño, I would have never had thought of the X-ray machine."

"Neither did the German, Paco. We are 1 and 0 right now. I need you guys to face down El Teco and the Rock Island Boys. If you guys are still on board, we have a job to do."

Jay leans back and pulls on his goatee. "Orale, I'm down. I want that feria in the case."

"Rigo, Paco?"

"We are in, Toño. Quit fucking around."

"Okay, boys, I'm going to call Freddy in San Antonio to find out where to pick up Chiquita."

"Oh, Chiquita? All right."

"Rigo, you do what you want with Chiquita. She never says no. But you treat her dirty, and she will plant you."

"We might need Freddy."

"Paco, I already have him on the back end, trailing us watching our six. I also hope to get Rick the Stick to take your spot on the glass."

"Why do they call him the Stick?"

"You never heard the story about Rick? They also call him Kentucky Windage."

The story goes he was somewhere he can't talk about years back with the best longshots and a lot of kills between them. Well, it started with who was the best long shooter. They decided to keep it fair, so they pulled out this old A2 bolt .30-06 from the armory with iron sights. Rick had first shot, so he loaded one round and pointed at a two-inch stick 300 meters past the 500-meter targets. Rick did his Kentucky windage about two or three inches above the stick and shook out a round. Two seconds after he shot, the stick exploded. Yeah, 800-meter shot with an unknown rifle and iron sights. Luck, maybe, but he shot with the best and won.

"Okay, let's see if I have the room covered for the job. It's us four and a ringer, two locals, a backend, and a stick shooter." I hand the case to Rigo. "You have the football, Mr. President."

"Toño, sometimes I have no idea what the hell you are talking about."

"The case is yours. Don't let it out of your sight." I wouldn't put it past some merc to do a stagecoach and try to rob us on the trail to Fort Worth. And that's the only reason I'm taking the chance in bringing my twin Glocks.

"I got it, but I am not handcuffing it to my wrist."

"Rigo, you did know what I was talking about—the football the president carries everywhere."

"I'm not stupid. I was just messing with you."

13

ON THE ROAD

Off on the trot, four smugglers in my Foringa King ranch truck. If we don't get stopped along the way, it will be only because my windows are so tinted. I call Freddy in San Antonio, and he gives me the pickup location at the famous Rebar Club in Alamo Heights, a neighborhood on the north side. Chiquita must have known I used to hang out at that snooty bar. I used to love to flaunt my career as a smuggler; the rich chicks like hanging out with bad boys, or they just hate their dad or something. I was new to the game back then and thought I was the shit. I had money and I was only 186 miles from home—far enough that my tio wouldn't find out what I was doing, but close enough to do a dash and be home in two hours and fifteen minutes.

It didn't always work out so well. One time at the Rebar, I must have been stirring a drink with the wrong rich girl and a dime was dropped. They don't like us criminal types rubbing up to the good girls of Alamo Heights. I learned the hard way that Alamo Heights has its own police department. If you're not from there, these cops go from "please, sir" to "you piece of shit" in a Nuevo Laredo second. They were four strong when they walked into the Rebar club. The bartender pointed me out with a nod. I had a couple of Blanton whiskeys while sitting next to Sissy, Lucy, Mary Ann—someone like that. I feel them home in and start flanking around me. Just before they dropped in with the "sir, we need to talk to you outside" bullshit, I stood up and yelled, "Check! I'm leaving San Antonio forever."

The bartender almost ran over, because he wasn't going to get the check paid after they pulled me outside. The bartender was a big, fat white boy with a shitty beard. "You owe me $150, slick."

The cops held back, watching, so I moved cautiously. I pulled out my gangster roll, peeled off two hundreds, and handed them to the fat boy. As he went to grab them, I pulled him close and whispered, "You shouldn't have done it. You are fucked, fat boy. Keep the change—you're going to need it."

The cops must have been making a point that night. They took me down right in the bar, cuffed and stuffed, dragging me out like a sack of melons. My truck was towed, and I slept in the cleanest jail I had ever seen. I bailed the next morning with a "drunk in public" charge, got my truck out of the pound, and limped home.

It was my fault; my tio always said that the only people impressed by smuggling are the cops. Fucking Alamo Heights—poor man's Dallas Highland Park.

14

SMUGGLER'S LESSON

Driving is a dangerous time because it allows you to second-guess every idea, plan, and outcome splashing in front of you. I said "splashing" because it begins to run every which way, like spilling whiskey on a marble bar. No matter which way you jump, you always manage to get some on you.

We blow by Laredo and pass Cotulla, Texas. The heat is shining off the hood of my truck, but it's cool enough for us river rats. The mesquite trees and cactus are everywhere without the river to look at. Texas is Texas, and I am a big fan of this patch of land. In Texas, if your word is good and you have a pair, you will do well. That is why I have always said it doesn't matter if you're white, brown, or red, it's who is stronger and willing to go that extra mile. My tío would say: "It's not what you deserve, but what you fight for." Texans are a bunch of fighters, and we are most dangerous when the chips are down and we're outnumbered.

I am constantly glancing at my crew for any facial expressions or murmurs of discontent. Paco is riding in the front. Rigo is sitting back right, with Jay on the left. He knows if we hit trouble, he covers the left side. The driver never shoots like in the movies. You try to do two things at once, you will end up upside down in a ditch. These are the things you learn in the Smuggler's Handbook of Life.

"Slow down, Toño, we are coming up to Pearsall."

"Jay, what do you know about Pearsall?" Rigo asks.

"I know you don't speed, spit, or piss in Pearsall. These cops are worse than the Laredo cops. They will take you to the can for any fucking reason."

"Pearsall cops? Really?"

"Paco, look around. All they have in this shithole is dirt and a minimum-security prison. I spent sixteen months in a cell here. Listen up, if you get pulled over for speeding and they find anything wrong, they will tow your car, confiscate what they can, and drag you to the justice of the peace. They don't play here—speeding, $200; no insurance, $200; broken taillight, $200. You catching my drift, homeboy? If you don't have the cash or a way to have it wired, they will take your watch, spare tire, even your leather jacket. They will take all your shit."

"They can't do that shit, Jay? That's bullshit, homes."

"No? Tell him, Toño."

"Rigo, here is the last place you want to get pulled over. They are not good cops, but vultures. My cousin, Sunny, got pulled over here. They took all his shit. They told him they were holding his Seamaster Omega watch and his spare tire as collateral. You guys know Sunny—he's a civilian, works sixty hours a week, and has three kids. Just think what they would do to us. I'll keep under the speed limit."

"Yeah, you do that, Toño. I just bought this Panerai Luminor watch."

"I noticed that, nice watch, Rigo. Whose wrist you snatch it off?"

"Sometimes you laugh at the wrong shit. I bought it at the jewelry store at the Mall Del Norte in Laredo for $8,995."

"Hey, Rigo, I'll give you fifty clams for it."

"Fuck you, Jay."

"Rigo, don't forget, that pinche high-end watch glows in the dark. Remember to tape it up or take it off if we do night work. It will give up our position."

"Toño, you don't take your Submariner off or tape it."

"It's a Rolex. You don't tape a Rolex. But a Panerai, well, why not."

Getting these guys to laugh and relax even for a minute is money. We are going to have a round or two with these Rock Island Boys, not knowing if we are getting played. The German is sinister and that makes his actions simple, but his thoughts complex. He never said the cartel wanted this piece of work to be done, nor did he mention El Commandante was involved. Who wants us in Fort Worth? The German must know I would bring a backup crew and have shadows like Freddy and Rick the Stick watching our backs. He knows we are holding a lot of cash, but what the hell am I supposed to bring back to him? Some box…containing what? Pinche German wants us in Funky Town early. We could do this drop in thirty minutes and be off on the roll.

I hope Snow White has some information. If that blonde, Finnish-born broad can't find out anything, nobody can. Hunter and Paesan should have our rooms ready and, knowing them, it's all going to be first class. The Farrier better be waiting for us at our room. I don't want my crew having nothing but rocks to chuck at the Rock Island Boys. Hunter will know if any word is on the street about our visit. If it gets out that we are having a sit-down with El Teco, believe it, Hunter will be running books on the odds of who will come out on top. They are all about the action and the money.

15

THE ALAMO HEIGHTS GIG

"Wake up! I need all your eyes."

"Why, Toño? Just go pick up Chiquita and let us sleep."

"Paco, I get lost in this city. Do I take 410 and loop the city, or go straight on down the gut on I-35?"

"You asking us, Toño"?

"One wrong move, boys, and we lose fifteen to thirty minutes, and we can't lose any time." I'm taking I-35 going down the belly of the beast, so, *I'm going to need these guys to start waking up.*

Rigo looks at Jay like he just got an idea. Jay starts hopping up and down like a kid wanting to go to the bathroom. "Jay, what's on your mind, homes?'"

"We need to eat, so why not stop at Mi Tierra for some menudo or mole? They're open 24/7."

"It's out of the way and parking sucks. And what if Chiquita wants to eat? I don't want to start with her pissed off."

Jay is a ruthless villain and will walk over bodies for a beer and good food. I also have to keep him happy or he will be a bitch to work with. "Mira, Jay, we might have some Alamo Heights vatos to deal with, and you know how we all are after we eat. Heavy, we all want to take a siesta, and we don't need to be slow on this roll. After we pick up Chiquita and bounce, Austin is only thirty minutes down the road. I'll take us to the best Mexican restaurant, Guero's."

"Guero's? I heard that place was the shit, but you get me to the Texas Chili Parlor, and we will be square."

"Hell yeah!" Rigo bellows with a big grin, rubbing his hands together.

"How about Paco?"

"Toño, I will eat anything other than Mexican food and chicken fried steak. I mean breakfast, lunch, and dinner they slap refried beans on your plate back home. Dude, beans for breakfast! I'm in on the Chili whatever."

Jay starts in. "Dude, they made a movie at that Chili Parlor and…."

As Jay entertains Paco and Rigo with his story of a movie and hot chili that feels like eating lava, I have to stay on point. I can't assume Freddy didn't plot a move using Chiquita as bait, or that they aren't working together. They know we are on a drop, which means we have cash or powder of some kind. I would say it's a 95 percent chance against it, but at times, the need is greater than honor. People do things against their nature for whatever reason, and that is what I was taught by my tio. Not so much by his words, but by his actions. He tried to kill me, his own nephew, to cover his tracks with the cartel. If he would do that to his own blood, then anybody can do it to anyone.

Driving down the center of San Antonio reminds me of why I hate big cities. The busy roads and big buildings are something. Street signs, asphalt, and cement kill your view. Forget about the noise; I guess you can get used to anything if you have to.

"Wachale! I can see the Alamo. We gave those white boys an ass-whipping that day! That's the Menger Hotel. It's haunted, bro."

"That's the Menger Hotel and bar all right. That is where Chiquita killed that dude in the upstairs corner."

"I heard she spilled him."

"What do you know about spilling, Rigo?"

"Paco, I hear things. Toño has done it. Tell him, Toño."

"My tio taught me the technique. He said the Japanese used to spill themselves as an honorable death. You need the right blade, longer than my Cold Steel, and you need to use muscle. You drive it in and plunge deep, cut across and up and across again. You better move fast after the last cut, or you will be painted in red. It's like walking with a big-ass bowl of menudo and pouring it on the floor in front of you. You never forget the splat."

"You know what, Toño, forget about Mi Tierra. Only you could fuck up my menudo craving."

"Jay, guys, let's get on point. We are on Broadway Street, crossing into Alamo Heights." The truck gets quiet and the work looks are back on—calm, still, and emotionless.

"Toño, it's on the right, dude. You drove right by it."

Jay pops up. "We are doing a dry run, Rigo. Don't want any surprises."

I take a tour of every building around the Rebar bar, looking for anything or anybody waiting for our visit. "Paco, you and Rigo go in first and cover the corners. And don't get in a crossfire this time."

"Ya, we got this. Give me the Glocks."

They were loaded by me, seventeen rounds in the mags and one in the pipe. I will go in a minute after they enter. It's 3:00 p.m., so it shouldn't be busy.

"If you see Chiquita, leave her alone. Don't talk to her. The back door is to the left of the bar. Keep an eye on it. If anybody is stupid enough to try a move, it will be from there. Jay, the truck is yours. If it turns to shit, we will go south, so set up and be ready to roll. When we leave, we will be going north toward the 410 Freeway. And keep an eye on the Pelican."

Jay just nods. He's an old pro and knows he can't keep up on a run for your life. He takes the wheel and I move back left.

Jay pulls up on a side street, and Rigo and Paco pop out and walk toward the Rebar bar. "Jay, when I bail, turn the truck around pointing south toward Broadway Street. Hopefully, we all walk out quiet-like, pulling Chiquita."

As I get out of the truck, Jay lowers his window to hear better.

"Hey, Jay, you think I'm crazy?"

"Toño, every morning I wake up and walk to my mailbox in my boxers and Jerusalem cruisers. One morning, I got up and had that feeling you have right now. I put on my khakis, shoes, and dress shirt. I slid my nickel .357 Colt Python in the front of my pants just to walk to the mailbox. I got to the mailbox and across the street is one of the Salazar brothers, sitting in a Toyota with his window down. I put my hand on my Python and he drove off. It's like you always say about guns—I'd rather have it."

"Jay, I think it's: *I'd rather have it and not need it than need it and not have it.*"

"No, Toño, I'd rather have it."

I walk off toward the Rebar, counting cars and looking for stickers like permit passes or IDs hanging from rearview mirrors or consoles. Nothing sticks out, everything looks local. You see, my crew thinks I'm worried about the cartel and the German. Maybe one of their soldiers is following the money and might try a play for the cash. It could happen. It would be a good play, but would the German believe us if we got rolled?

But no, I'm worried that the people looking for Chiquita will roll up as we pick her up. Murphy's Law and all that. She's vulnerable because people know where she is. People clone, copy, and capture cell calls all day long for the right price. And not knowing who she killed puts us at a disadvantage. That's my fault. I should have made some calls on who is hunting Chiquita, just didn't have the time.

We have the corners of the bar covered with Glocks, and I have my Cold Steel knife—I can touch anyone within twenty-one feet. Inside that, you won't clear leather. Paco has the back left, and Rigo is covering the front right. We have Jay pointing south and, knowing Jay, he will use my truck to run people over if we end up moving to the parking lot.

I pull the door open and that smell hits me—money bar. I stop just inside to let my eyes adjust to the dimly lit bar. I take three steps and Rigo is in the right corner. I notice three older men at the bar and a couple sitting at a table. The Mexican couple is facing the bar. The guy is in his mid-twenties, bland, long-sleeved shirt probably covering his tattoo sleeves. I know this because it's 105 degrees outside. The girl is thirtyish, but she's been ridden hard and put away wet, never seeing a drop of saddle soap. They have two drinks—not bar drinks, but Whataburger paper cups.

I look behind the bar and there is bad luck fat boy with that shitty beard that dropped the dime on my last visit. Paco sits in the back-left corner, facing everyone and smiling. He nods to the end of the bar. The back corner has a blind spot where the shelves stick out enough to hide a small girl's head.

Just about then, Chiquita leans forward, looking across the room and not picking me out. Right then, I know she's waiting for me to do the calling when I'm ready. She leans back and disappears from my vision, but not Paco's.

I walk to the bar and the fat, clueless bartender walks over with a, "What do you want?"

"Your head on a stick," I retort.

Fat boy looks up with some attitude. "What the…." Now he recognizes me. "Hey, man, I'm sorry. I didn't know who you were. Freddy came by and had a chat with me. The son of a bitch dislocated my shoulder here at the bar."

"Shut the fuck up, fat boy. Lean back and don't move till I leave." After a long pause, I add, "Or I will kill you."

The fat boy leans back and sticks his hands in his pockets. I turn away from the bar and face the couple in the center of the room with their backs to the wall.

I raise my two index fingers and touch them in front of my face. Paco and Rigo move like arrows from each corner of the room with Glocks at the ready, pointing them at the couple. We have them in a position that is useless to resist. The couple is seasoned, because they place their palms on the table and become statues. Seeing this, Paco and Rigo take seats cornering the couple, with the Glocks on the table and hands on the Glocks. I walk up between the brothers and stand there staring at the girl, waiting for her to talk.

She looks up and simply says, "Freddy has us covering Chiquita."

"Prove it, or we will leave you here, you understand me?"

Rigo and Paco grip the Glocks aggresively to make my point.

"Freddy showed us a picture of you and him bird hunting in Mexico. Both of you were holding a bird by the wings."

"What was the color of my shirt?"

"You had a vest on, but no shirt."

I back up, leaving Paco and Rigo babysitting. I walk by the older gentlemen at the bar that are just staring at their drinks, not moving. They understand they are in the middle of a Mexican standoff, and I bet they're hoping they don't become collateral damage. I hold my hands up to show Chiquita I come as friend.

"Toño, you still covering all your bases like your tio."

"Chiquita, you know the two with my boys?"

"I came in and they trailed me. They blocked my exit, so they had me in a barrel. I thought the best thing to do was sit and wait for my South Texas river rats from my esquina."

"They said Freddy sent them to cover you."

"Freddy! He does treat me like his sister, but that doesn't sound like him."

"Let me text him, Chiquita. Don't use yours, people are tracking you, and I bet they smell blood."

I text him: *Why the shadow?*

He answers: *What shadow?*

I look up and Chiquita has the "oh shit" look.

"Chiquita, the guy you spilled—was he white or Mexican?"

"White, why?"

"You packing?"

"Shit, yeah, Toño."

"Draw your pistol and come up over my left shoulder to cover the old guys at the bar."

"Why?"

"Do it now."

Like clockwork, she pops up with a .380 cal Beretta cocked and off safety. I turn, look at Rigo, and then dart my eyes to the three sixty-year-old-plus men at the bar. Rigo glides to the front door with his pistol zeroed in on them.

Paco stands over the couple, covering them and us at the bar. Boy, I could use a Glock right about now.

The men are motionless, but their demeanor is that of battle-tested military men. How did I miss it? They are doing everything backward. Sitting together, the same age, and dressed very San Antonio. These others were decoys and cover for these guys. Their clothes and backs to the wall, with Whataburger cups on the table. My tio would give me a slap for missing the clues. They are always there to be found; you just have to get over the obvious. We have the room and they know it. It is completely covered, and Chiquita is sitting behind the sight of a Beretta.

I turn my attention to the gentlemen at the bar. "What war? Hey, what war?"

The one closest to me murmurs, "Vietnam."

"Place your hands on the bar, or let's go to war."

They reluctantly place their hands on the bar. I can tell that they are not professionals to the trade but have spilled blood.

"By the looks of things, you boys and the couple behind me were going to snatch Chiquita and play a little catch up for what she did. Now, I'm guessing the guy she dropped like a rock is a relation. Maybe a grandson to one of you guys?"

The one in the middle looks up and gives me a look of pure hate.

Right about then, I hear sniffling. The bartender is face-down on the dirty floor with his hands over his head, crying it up. This makes me smile.

"You guys had your chance, but now we have you in the barrel, as they say. You in the middle, you can think about it.

But remember, you will be responsible for killing your war buddies over something you can't change. We have business elsewhere and Chiquita is coming with us.

"Listen up, cabrones! She is now under the protection of the South Texas Mafia. My name is Toño. Anything happens to Chiquita, there will be no place for you or yours to hide. We will kill you and wipe your family from existence. Your grandson fucked with the wrong people and got clipped. Bad things happen. Don't make them worse."

The other gentlemen look at their friend like "what did you get us into?"

"Stand up nice and easy, gentlemen."

They stand up and are followed by the sound of metal hitting the floor; they had pistols sitting on their laps. I go behind them and pick up three of the prettiest Colt 1911 .45 cal. pistols I have ever seen. All loaded and cocked, ready for action. I lower the hammers on all three, place two in my front pockets, and keep one in hand at the ready.

All three men have one pant leg pulled over their right boot. I tap the boots with my foot to make sure they don't have an extra throw-down pistol.

"Sit down, boys, and I will get back with you." I turn my attention to the couple behind me. I cock the .45 in my hand and level it on the girl. "Where are your guns?"

"In his boot and my bag."

I grab the girl's bag and pull out a MAC-10 9mm semiautomatic—a real piece of shit. I unload it, drag the mag out, and place it on the table next to them. I walk over and take the guy's gun out of his boot. It's a .38 cal. nickel S&W Chief Special revolver. "What were you going to do with this, piss us off?"

I unload it and twist the screw holding the cylinder. I take the cylinder off and throw it across the room. I grab the MAC-10 magazine and bend the mouth so it can't feed the bullets.

"Did you two hear what I said to the gentleman at the bar?"

"Yes."

"Chiquita, let's go." She grabs her purse and she's off toward the door. I stop her and tell her Jay is in my truck and to sit on the back left.

"Gentlemen, these are fine weapons, and I'm sure you've earned them. Give me twenty minutes after we leave, and I will drop your pistols off for you."

I hear whimpers from Rigo and Paco.

"How you going to do that, return our property?"

"I will drop them in the dumpster by the carwash up the street. Fair enough? All three nod with sighs of relief. "Oh, and I thank you for your service."

I fade back with Rigo and Paco backing out after me. Jay has backed up the truck almost to the front door. We all casually walk out, hop in, and off we go—four South Texas river rats and our ringer.

16

THE DASH FOR THE PARLOR

"Holy shit, Toño, what just fucking happened?"

"Jay, the carwash is up ahead. Pull up to the back dumpster."

Rigo hands me a Church's Fried Chicken bag, as Jay pulls up to the car so I can dump these pistols.

"Chingado, Toño, they are beautiful, homes."

"I know, right? They are engraved with Vietnam shit all over them."

"I want them, Toño."

"Jay, I can't. They belong to three soldiers that fought in the war."

Jay slows just enough; I toss the bag with the pistols in the dumpster. "Chiquita, hand me your pistol. Hurry."

"What? Fuck you, Toño, I will be at the mercy of my enemies and you guys."

I turn and glare at her. "Give me the Beretta."

She reluctantly hands it over. I drop it in the dumpster, and off we go.

Jay pops it north, then east on Hwy. 410, then north again on I-35. He looks at me with disgust and says, "Man, I hate your ass."

I laugh and look back at Rigo and Paco. They break out in laughter, relieved.

Chiquita is just sitting with her arms crossed, pissed off about her pistol. "Well, what took you guys so long?"

Then we all start really laughing out loud.

"Okay, Jay, I will tell you what happened. We had two decoys, three simple snatchers, and a crybaby."

"Okay, I got it."

"Toño, how did you know the two by the wall were decoys?"

"Mira, Rigo, I figured it out after I texted Freddy and he didn't know who the couple was. I ran the room in my mind, and the couple gave it away with the Whataburger cups. You can't bring drinks into bars, 'specially this snobby bar. That fat bartender should have told them to get rid of them. Then, they had their backs to the wall. I put it together when Chiquita told me the guy she stabbed was a white boy. And, I remembered that Freddy had also said the guys that pressed him seemed like family non-pros. That's when I really studied the three old guys—they were too calm, just staring at their drinks. Then, I noticed all their hands were under the bar. A couple more seconds and they might have made a move. We got lucky.

"When Rigo moved to the door, we had them flanked, so they knew it was over. Chiquita had them covered with the gun she used to have."

"Fuck you, Toño, just fuck you!"

Rigo looks at Chiquita and says, "He will buy you another one."

"I will, Chiquita."

"He will buy you a better one, with a gold trigger and mep sights."

My look tells Rigo to shut the hell up. "Yeah, Chiquita a better one."

"You better, because I am pissed off."

"Hey, Toño, I liked that speech you laid on them. What was that you called us, South Texas Mafia?"

"You liked that, Paco? Not bad, right? I even scared myself."

Jay is driving with that lost look on his face. "Speech? What, you had to give a 'you never want to see me again' talk?"

Rigo jumps in. "Yeah, what was it, we will kill and burn everything on earth or something like that?"

"That's not what I said or how I said it. Think they bought it? Chiquita, what do you think?"

"Damn, Toño, I believed it, and looking at them—they did, too. But what was all that—South Texas Mafia?"

"It's just sauce for the enchiladas."

I have three deep in the backseat, and I'm damn glad to have them. The problem is, Chiquita has the window and Rigo is sitting bitch. I can see him fidgeting. It's just a matter of time.

"Chiquita, can we switch seats? You know, boy, girl, boy?"

Chiquita gives Rigo a sexy look. "Who said you were a boy?"

After a laugh, the begging begins. "Please, please do this for me and I will owe you one."

"Okay, cabron, I will sit bitch for that. Remember you will owe me one."

"Yeah, but a small one, not a big one."

"No such thing, Rigo. You will owe me one, or else." Chiquita is smiling and Rigo is finally comfortable, looking out the window.

I finally have the time to take a good look at Chiquita. She's wearing a pair of cool black lace-up boots with her black pants tucked inside. A coin belt and a low-cut, long-sleeved, tight-fitting pullover. She's thirty-five or so, but can pass for twenty-five with her smooth, caramel skin and big, brown eyes. Her black hair is pulled up for war.

"Hey, Toño, what are you looking at?"

I nod at her boots. "Michael Kors?"

"No, they're Vince. Now quit looking at me. You had your shot and you blew it."

Rigo can't help himself. "So, Toño blew you?"

Chiquita wheels around and hits Rigo's shoulder with a right cross. When she connects, we all flinch—what a punch. Rigo shakes and turns with a painful smile to stare out the window. He's rubbing his shoulder.

"Okay, Toño, you guys saved my ass from those body snatchers, so I'm yours. What is the play, who are we jiving with, and who is the mark?"

"You heard of the South Texas drag we did?"

"Yeah, everybody did. You guys outplayed the Mexican Cartel and El Commandante. Legendary."

"Did you know they missed my tio and El Machete?"

"Yeah, so?"

"Since we became the lead in South Texas, the Cartel has been real careful using us. I can't blame them, but we are big earners and never miss a drop or a pickup, and we are three steps ahead of Johnny Law."

"So, what, Toño? Just spit it out."

Paco and Rigo are looking at me like I'm telling them a goodnight story where they are the heroes.

"Well, we got put on this drop and roll with a meet and greet in Fort Worth. So here lies the problem, mi chiquita. The German called me in personally to meet with him and his mercs in Guerrero, Mexico to give me this piece of work. I thought I was going to end up in a fifty-five-gallon drum outside the city limits.

"The German tells me to take that case next to you to Fort Worth. He wants me to meet with a guy named El Teco and his Rock Island Boys and drop the case. I'm to return a box and place it at the German's feet. He didn't say where. The German also told me what was in the case—money—but not to open it."

"You fucking opened it, right? I might be sitting next to a bomb?"

"Relax, Chiquita we had the case X-rayed. It is money, lots of it."

"You met with the German? What was he wearing?"

"Damn, he really looked good. Like a young Peter O'Toole."

"Well, you know they don't expect you to make it back. But after what I saw back at the Rebar, you have a good chance. I've never seen any crew cover a room like your guys did. Moved without thinking or hesitation, and, more important, held the room: five tangos with two Glocks and a calm voice. Now I know why the Mexican Cartel still uses you. I would rather have you as a friend than an enemy. I do think if you make it back with the box, the German will assassinate you. Then he will pick off your crew one at a time."

Jay swerves. "Damn, Chiquita, tell us what you really think."

Chiquita is right; this cake has a lot of layers. We have to start thinking like we did at the Rebar. Let's not take what is obvious as gospel. My tio once said: "Don't do anything unless there is money in it." Where is the money in having us clipped by the Rock Island Boys or having us drop El Teco and his crew?

"Chiquita, I'm going to put you on El Teco's brother, Roberto. He was a bigshot politician, but El Teco fucked that up for him. Roberto is a bigtime gambler now. I will have my two locals sit you next to him. I need you to find out anything he knows about this drop."

"I can do that, but I've been in the wind for weeks. I will need to run to Neiman's or Saks. Baby needs better bait!"

"Chiquita, will you marry me?"

Chiquita draws back to punch Rigo again.

"Just kidding, girl, don't hit me."

"Toño, this isn't a usual drop and roll, you know that. El Teco is known to be a crazy psycho. He thinks he can't be killed. He's in some kind of cult—Palo Mayombe, I think. Like that shit that happened in Matamoros, eating human hearts and brains. Sick shit."

That makes sense; when we met him days back in Zapata, he had that "I'm el diablo, invincible" thing going on.

"Chiquita, you know Snow White? She's the white version of you."

"I've heard of her. Why don't you put her on Roberto?"

"He knows her colorful past in Funky Town. I have her pumping the Rock Island Boys for any information about our meet. I might need you as a ringer. We will insist on a public place for the meet, so I might need you in the crowd as our unknown. I'm going to have the two local boys, Hunter and Paesan, pick you up at the old Rig Restaurant off I-35."

"How do you know these locals? Have you worked with these two guys, and do you trust them?"

"I have and I do, Chiquita. They are pros and won't leave you high and dry. Good enough? You will like them. Hunter looks like Telly Savalas, and Paesan is a knock-around guy from New York. But remember, you're engaged to Rigo."

Chiquita just nods and relaxes. She knows I wouldn't vouch for them if they weren't the real deal.

"Once they pick you up, you will go through them with any information passed to us. I'm sure we will be trailed once we hit downtown. They will tell you where the meet will be. Tell them what hardware you need, and we will get the Farrier to suit you up. Here's 2,000 dollars for your new duds."

"Two thousand dollars? That's it?"

"Make it versatile and sexy—two blouses and one pair of pants. Use your badass Vince boots."

"They are the Monastir Vince boots, Toño."

"I don't know what is going to go down, so get all the information you can. If something happens to us, hit the wind. If we get dropped, I've worked it out so you get paid. My maid will drop letters in the mail and get you your slice."

"Toño, how can a simple drop and roll get so fucked up? Maybe it is a simple move."

"If I thought like that, you would be tied to a chair and we would be dead. Jay would have a new truck, so that's one ray of sunshine."

He throws his hair back over his shoulder. "Damn right, I like this Foringa pick 'em up."

I roll back in my seat and drift off in thought. A lunch at the Chili Parlor in Austin, then two and a half hours to arrive and rain pain on those Rock Island Boys. We have the edge in this game. We are the unknowns, we don't flinch, and we see past most setups, and that's the best thing on our side. Another thing is that El Teco is insane, and that puts him at a disadvantage. Instead of us being worried, we need to start getting them to worry. I know how to take a leg out and lean on them.

17

KEEP AUSTIN WEIRD

Austin, Texas, city of Gomorrah. If you can't get laid in Austin, you can't get laid. Don't have time to visit our old friend, Shitty, at his Dirty Dog Bar. We will never make Fort Worth, so we move on to the Chili Parlor. I wonder if El Commandante's daughter, Lorraine/Miss UT, ever stopped by to get her free drink. The chatter starts from the backseat.

"Toño, damn, let's eat."

"Rigo, we are on our way to the Parlor. Jay, when you get to Sixth Street, get off and go all the way to Lavaca and turn right.

"I don't want to go to the Chili Parlor."

"Have you ever been to the Chili Parlor, Chiquita?"

"No, I have not, but it sounds like a shithole."

"Chiquita we are going to the Parlor, ya basta!"

"Okay, Jay, but they better have good burgers."

"Toño, tell her about the Parlor."

"The food is killer. It's better than Mama's in San Antonio, and a movie with that director was made in that place."

"What guy? You guys are lying."

"It's that guy with a big chin like Jay Leno."

"What movie?"

"The one with the blacked-out Nova, I don't remember the name. The Parlor has real good food, and if you like hot chili, this is the place." I can tell everyone is way too tired to argue. A couple of turns and we get the front spot—our luck is changing.

"Rigo."

"Yeah, I have the football, Mr. President."

"Okay, we go in, order our food, eat, and leave. No whiskey, Jay, we have to stay frosty."

We walk in and it's empty except for some barflies. We take the table by the kitchen, facing the door just in case. Just about then, I hear somebody yell, "Big T!" Mario Cadillac is working the bar today. He's a big, biker-looking dude with a black beard.

"Mario C., que paso, ese! Long time no see, you been doing time or what?"

"Not me."

"Mario, how is that antique Caddy of yours?"

"How do you think? It's at the shop, but it is shining and profiling."

"It's good to see you, but we are in a dash and we need to be on the roll in thirty minutes. Can you help us out, brother?"

"Orale, I'll press the cook and have the waitress over to your table a la volada. Hey, Toño, thank you for that thing you did with that guy last year."

"Hey, you're Mario C., don't worry about it. It was my pleasure, my friend."

I get back to the table as my crews are ordering. "I'll have the burger and potato salad and iced tea."

"No fries?"

"Rigo, you have never had potato salad like this. I think they have a German lady make it for them. It will make your toes curl worse than Chiquita."

All four yell out, "Potato salad!"

We all eat like we are in juvie—fast before the big kids take our food. The secret in juvenile hall was to spit on your food to make sure nobody would take it. Some things you just can't forget. The waitress comes back with the bill and lets us know Mario C. has taken care of it.

"Jay, don't say it."

"Why not? Crime don't pay."

"Let's load up and roll. Jay, you still up to drive?" He just gives me that pachuco look, head leaned back, eyes squinted, and an upside-down smile. "I'll catch up with you guys, I need to have words with Mario C."

Mario walks to the corner by the kitchen, where there is a creepy poster of a clown that's been there forever.

"Mario, if any of my crew come in in the next couple of days, give them any help you can. I will square it times two, my word."

"Sure, Toño. You expecting problems?"

"What do you think? I will see you when I see you. Good luck with that '50s Cadillac."

I always have a safety valve just in case we have to hit the mattresses, as they used to say. Nobody in our world knows Mario C., and he owes me one.

I love the Chili Parlor, but it's time to hit the road. I jump in the passenger side of my truck and off we go. Jay gives me a sorry-ass look and points to the backseat. All three are dead to the world. Chiquita is leaning on Paco; she knows he's more of a gentleman than Rigo, who would sneak a feel.

"You see, Jay, that's why I didn't want you guys to eat at Mi Tierra before we picked up Chiquita. Mira los, they are useless."

"Why would you even know that, Toño? You're a weird dude."

"I have never been told that. We have two hours and thirty minutes to go in this traffic, so picale."

"Toño, I give you shit, but I trust you and the moves you make. You better figure out the backside of this drop and roll. I've been around, but this simple move has turned out to have more moves than Ex-Lax."

"Ex-Lax! Ex-Lax, Jay, really?"

"You ever take Ex-Lax? It goes everywhere. It's just you and me driving two and a half hours before we hit the hornets' nest. Run it down. What would your uncle, El Maestro, do?"

My tio was everything to me. When my dad died, he went from Uncle to Dad. At first, he was cool. Then, he brought me into his crew. By the time I was a senior in high school, I was running most of his smuggling routes from Brownsville to Big

Ben country. I handled air, water, and tunnels. Hell, it was my idea to use a catapult to cross the loads over the stupid fence. I studied what the dogs hated and came up with a coffee and Mexican mole mix that drug dogs ignore.

He taught me everything about the worst things, but nothing about the good things. He tried to turn me into El Machete, a fat Mexican with no conscience. When he could not, and an opportunity arose, he made the move to have me killed, and that is why we are here today. He ripped off the Mexican Cartel and set us up for the fall, but we outplayed El Maestro and the cartel. How my tio pulled a Houdini and escaped the Mexican Cartel still hasn't played out. The last thing he said to me: "Remember, I taught you all you know, but not all I know."

"Toño, I'm not stupid, even though everybody thinks I am. We didn't beat the cartel, kidnap the Commandante's daughter, play with the German, return the girl, escape death in every corner, and end up in Yucatan without help."

"You trust me, Jay?" I stare at him with a calm, calculating look.

He leans back with a bewildered look. Suddenly, a light turns on and he just smiles. Some things are better left unsaid.

18

THE LOCAL BOYS

The drive up I-35 is quiet and traffic is light. I have to get it right in my head. We just can't handle even one misstep in the dance. Like it has been said: "One slip of the tongue and you're in deep shit." Time to wake the dead in the backseat.

"Hey, Toño, you want me to slam on the brakes?"

"If it weren't my truck, I would say yes. You know how much a brake job costs. Rigo, Paco!"

Rigo yells out, "Ready, ready, boss, we are up!"

"Paco, wake Chiquita up. She's slobbering all over my leather seat."

Paco gives me a scared look. "No, you wake her up."

"I'm not scared to wake her up. Jay, tap the brakes a couple times."

Just about then we hear from Chiquita. "I'm up, chicken shit."

Rigo asks, "Where is your left hand, girl?"

She pulls out a four-and-a-half-inch blade and just smiles.

"I'm going to contact Hunter and Paesan to make sure they are at the pickup."

"I'm taking your word these two guys are up for the challenge."

"I have something to say to you, Chiquita. If we get in a barrel and you see it's useless for a backdoor ringer rescue, don't. Slip away and vanish."

"Ay, Toño, you worried about me? Don't be. I'm on the spot and I can yank and pop with the best. I'll be there when you need me."

"Esta bien, I just had to say it."

"I know how you're always playing the tough river rat smuggler, but I have seen the other side."

"You have two sides, Toño?"

"I only have one side, Rigo, and now I have to get the locals for the pickup. Time flies when an ex-girlfriend is grilling you."

I tell Jay to get off two exits up and turn left over I-35. The old Rig Restaurant is on the left.

"What are they driving?"

"Hunter and Paesan will be in a black Ford four-door pickup. It has a Harley Davidson package. It should be backed up in the back of the building. Stop short of the building and park."

"Toño, why are we out in the open? Let's go to the back and meet them. We're exposed," Chiquita says.

"Paco, talk to her, will you please?"

"Never go to them, Chiquita, let them come to you. If it was a hit, would you rather be in there like fish in a barrel blocked left, right, and forward, or out here in the open where we can flee popping on the roll?"

"You motherfuckers are good."

Just then, here comes the black pickup; I see Hunter driving, and Paesan is shotgun. They stop just short of my truck. Paesan gets out and waits for me to meet him.

"Toño, you want a Glock?"

"No, I got this. They're on our side of the fight."

I get out and walk over to Paesan. He has his hair all slicked back, a tight Affliction shirt unbuttoned to his navel, and a silver chain with a cross dangling. Just like a Gumba! Hunter waves and stays on point in the truck, keeping an eye out for trouble.

"Yo, how you doing, Toño?"

"Paesan, my little Italian, give me a squeeze. I'm sending Chiquita with you guys. Set her up in a room. She will need some things. She is very important to the work at hand. You think you can plant her next to El Teco's brother, Roberto?"

"What do you think? I have him in a game we are running in Diamond Hill tonight. I can put my hands on him anytime."

"I might just need him later. I see Hunter is always watching out for the ambush."

"Hunter is Hunter. He is not going to change for you or anybody. He has that third eye, you know."

"Yeah, in his ass."

"You have everything set up. The Farrier is waiting for you guys at your hotel."

"Where we staying?"

"Your favorite place. You have the same suite you had last time."

Nice. I wave to Hunter to thank him for the suite; he just gives me a nod. "Tell Hunter to pick me up by the back door of the hotel in two hours. I need him to show me some places for the meet and greet and the drop and roll. Get Chiquita whatever she needs—clothes but I will get her the hardware. Anything else you guys work out is your own business."

"Yeah, I heard what she did to that guy at the Menger bar. I don't need that kind of bad after me."

Chiquita jumps out, smiling at Paesan, and trots to backseat of Hunter's truck.

Paesan just gives me a smile and says, "No, I do not, Toño."

"You better watch your ass, Paesan, Chiquita will eat you alive." I walk back to the truck with the original villains in Funky Town. "Jay, drive us back up I-35 and go downtown. We're staying at the Ashton. It's the best place to stay for this kind of trip."

The Ashton is the coolest hotel in Fort Worth. The management charges us a chunk of money to turn a blind eye to what goes on. They allow villains, like the Farrier, to come in with all his boxes and set up his wares in the room. They also have a veterinarian that can come in to pull a bullet, stop bleeding, and provide pain pills if needed.

"Park the truck in the alley. They have a spot for us by the back door."

"How the fuck do you know all this shit, Toño?"

"My tio helped the owner with several power plays made by some very nasty elements. The fat Machete earned his money on that job. Since then, every villain in Texas and Mexico stays at the Ashton."

"What about El Teco? He would know about this place. Won't they call him?"

"I'm counting on it, Rigo. I'm actually asking them to let him know."

All three just look at me and shake their heads in amazement.

"Jay, the hotel is on the left. Drive by the north end, turn right, and park by the kitchen. Every Tex-Mex can find the kitchen. Back the truck up by the back door."

"That's too obvious, Toño."

"I know, Jay, that's the point."

We walk in through the kitchen and out to the lobby. An older white lady is standing behind the desk with her arms crossed. I tell her we have reservations.

"Under what name?"

"Mr. Smith."

"Mr. Smith, your suite is ready."

"Thank you, Beverly. Could you sign me in please, and if somebody asks if we are in town, please feel free to let them know."

"Your keys, Mr. Smith. Enjoy your stay. The Farrier is waiting in your suite. And please remember, the business stays outside."

"Of course, Beverly. Nothing comes to visit at the Ashton."

We exit the elevator and the floor is ours. The management won't rent any rooms while we are here. They can't afford any trouble. The guys are acting like they've never been out of Zapata. I can tell my crew feels out of their element.

"Boys, it's all good. You guys are acting like you've never been in the mixer."

They all buck up, and the attitude returns. It's funny how a simple thing like terrain changes your confidence. When I was outside of my element, my tio would always say: "You know, fear, blood, and death are the same in Zapata as they are in Paris. Treat it the same, or you will lose your edge."

Jay throws open the door to the three-bedroom suite. We all look like kids in *Willie Wonka*—the original one with Wilder, not Depp. In the middle of the room is an old Texican with an even older assistant next to him. If you saw them walking down the street, you wouldn't give them a second look. They look like retired city workers wearing plain, brown slacks, brown, button-down shirts, and cowboy boots. Ah, but their boots are handmade by Fort Worth's Rod Patrick—I can tell his handiwork a mile away. If I had the time, I would have him make me a pair of sharkskin. Someday, I hope.

On the bed is a sheet covering all our tools. The Farrier folds the sheet back and exposes a bed full of rifles, shotguns, pistols, and edge weapons. With his deep Spanish accent, he barks, "Please, see what will fit your needs."

Rigo grabs two 92F 9mm Berettas and four magazines. Paco goes with the reliable Browning Hi-Power 9mm pistol with five magazines and an MP5 submachine gun, the more compact executive model. The Browning pistol doesn't have the capacity of the Glock or Beretta, but it's accurate.

Jay grabs a four-inch Nickel .357 Colt Python with a handmade grip and, because he will likely be driving, he takes the Benelli Semiauto 12-gauge shotgun with the pistol grip. You can tilt that shotgun left and fire all seven shots before the first shell hits the ground; it can make the mess we just might need.

I pick out another MP5 with two stacked magazines and four magazines for my Glocks.

"Señor, I will need these two .380 cal. Beretta's with the four magazines, as well."

"For who?"

We all freeze and look at each other. "Bueno, Señor, who needs to know?"

"Este, I see everything you gentleman picked out fit you. I just wanted to fit whomever might need the Berettas."

"There is nobody else—these are to stash in locations in case we get patted down. You know, like the pistol in the crapper in *The Godfather.*"

"Please excuse my question. This is a private affair, and it must stay that way or I am out of business."

Is it an innocent question by the Farrier or is he trying to find out intelligence for El Teco? We can't take the chance on letting anybody know who we have working with us.

"I will have a talk with management about your question. Anything happens and they will have a word with you. Get out and leave those two duffle bags." I hand the Farrier a white envelope that he does not dare to open. He lowers his head and leaves with his toolbox in tow.

"You think the Farrier will drop a dime on us, Toño?"

"Well, Rigo, they know or will know we are in town, and they will know what hardware we have. Believe it or not, it will give us an edge."

I tell Paco and Rigo to tear down the weapons and make sure they have firing pins and springs in the magazines, and that the barrels aren't blocked. I don't trust the Farrier after his question.

"You got it, boss."

"Remember, boys—measure twice, cut once."

"Toño, they know we are here and what hardware we have. How does that help us?"

"Yeah, they do, Jay, but that needed to happen. We need them to think they have us. They're expecting four river rat smugglers that are out of their element. They will let us pick the meet and greet location without too much trouble, because they think they're controlling the game. Most crews will set up an hour or two early before the meet. These guys won't, because they know where we are, and they will have eyes on us and follow us to the meet. At the meet, El Teco will be a dick and fuck with me. Don't let him get to you—it's a war, not a battle."

"And?"

"That's all I got so far, Rigo, but we will be ready by the meet."

"Toño, I trust you, but, dude, it's a little late in the game for Hail Marys."

"Listen, guys, raptors, think like raptors—they hunt in packs. When the hunter thinks he has a raptor dead in his sights, the hunter turns into the hunted. The bait is set, and they hit the hunter from the blind side. Nothing is what it looks like, and we are the unknowns. Let's let them think they have us in a barrel."

"Rigo, how are the weapons?

"Tiptop, all in working order."

"Okay, I am going to slip out and meet Hunter. Move the curtain once in a while to let them know we are in the room."

"You have a way to get out undetected?"

"This place has a basement that comes out behind the hotel. Hunter is picking me up there in fifteen minutes."

"You're a smooth cat, Toño."

Let's not start jacking off each other just yet. We need to find a place for the meet and greet and drop and roll, along with an exit plan. Get some rest and order in. The food is good here. The only person allowed to come up here is that older blonde you guys saw at the front desk, Beverly. If it's not her or she has anybody with her, it's a hit, so be careful."

"Why would they do that?"

"Rigo, think about it. We are in a room with the money. If they can get us with our guard down, they get the money, but not without consequences. I don't think they would do it, but it is an option, I'm just saying. So, stay frosty."

HUNTER'S DRIVE

S lip, slide, and out the back, quiet and smooth. A peek, and there is the black pickup on a slow roll. Hunter knows enough to lower all the windows so I know what I am stepping into. He is staring straight ahead. I pop in, windows go up. What's next, I have no idea.

"You like the room?" Hunter is known for wearing suits on a daily basis, even in this heat.

"Off the rack, Hunter?"

He just gives me a look. "I have my own tailor."

"Nice, is that wool?"

"Linen, because of this damn heat. Now, let's get to it. I have a date."

"You always have a date. Let me guess, another redhead? And yes, the room is perfect, brother."

"Paesan has Chiquita ready for a sit with El Teco's brother tonight. The Rock Island Boys don't like to stray too far from their hood. I have a couple of places I will drive you by for the drop and roll. I was thinking the Mercury Chophouse for the initial meet, but you need to have the location for the drop and roll before you set the meet. Your shadow will have to improvise after he sees the Rock Island Boys' setup."

"If we use the Mercury Chophouse, can you get Zack to put my guy in the kitchen?"

"Sure, great idea."

"Rick the Stick can set himself up with his rifle to cover everything outside the restaurant. Who can tell him what to do or how to do it?"

"Snow White has been on the task for the past day. That blue-eyed bombshell can get the devil to eat ice. So, when she tells me that there is no word about you guys being on a roll in Funky Town, I believe her. She did say the mid-level soldiers are edgy and know—or were told to be—ready. But South

Texas, you, or a drop and roll with a meet and greet were not even talked about. Not even the old 'I can't talk about it, wink, wink.' She wanted to know if you needed her for cover or as a beard."

"Keep her close. We might need her."

"Toño, if this was just a simple drop, why would they be so secret about it? I know my town, but this—this shit you're doing has an out-of-town feel to it. My advice is to walk away."

I tell Hunter that's what we do. We don't have the luxury of picking out jobs, but we do have the smarts to play our opponents. "It's done, Hunter, so let's get to the job."

Hunter can't possibly understand what me and my crew have been through. We were recruited at a young age at gunpoint. We have done shit we aren't proud of, but as we get older and start having more control of our lives, we get smarter and tougher. If we stay together as a crew, the Mexican Cartel, El Commandante, and even the German won't want to mix it up with us. Hunter chose his slice of the crime world, as did Paesan. They can always walk away; we can't.

Hunter drives by several places for the drop and roll, and we find a perfect one: Fred's Texas Cafe. We have several South Texas Valley boys that work in the kitchen, so we now have an edge.

"Okay, Hunter, I need to know what Chiquita finds out in real time ASAP. She has to be tied to Roberto at the hip. You tell her this is important, and to do whatever she has to do to corner that rabbit."

"Come on, man, she's a nice chick."

"I'm not asking. If I told her to gut you like a pig, she would do it on the quick, so don't get confused. That's why she's such a good ringer. You're a well-dressed, casino-running, shylock. We work for the Mexican Cartel as slaves. We are drug smuggling killing machines if we are placed in that position— and we are being placed in that position, slick."

"I have to keep it in mind who you guys are and why you South Texas runners are here. I won't make that mistake again."

"Groovy. Now, take me back to the Ashton."

Hunter pulls in to the back alley and stops. I yank the two .380 Berettas and magazines from the small of my back. "Hunter, give these to Chiquita. Paco checked them out and they're good to go."

Hunter opens his armrest and drops them in. "I'm not sure if I want to give them to Chiquita now."

I roll out with a smile. It's nice to have locals, but they have never seen the actual monsters that we deal with.

20

THE MEET

"What the hell did you guys order?" The suite is full of room service trays.

"Hey, we were hungry, bro!"

"Four hours, be ready for a meet." They go silent and the mood changes from hot to cold. "I'm going to make some calls, so get your minds right. Rest, sleep, whatever you need to do, but be on task in four."

I call Freddy first, because I know Rick the Stick is already in town. "Hey, Fred! Are you in Fort Worth?"

"Thirty minutes out."

"Good, here's what I need. The meet is in four hours at Zack's place. You know him—he owns the Mercury Chophouse. Go straight over there and apron up. Just tell Zack it's a favor I'm calling in. He owes me one.

"Don't tell me you never worked in a kitchen. You're going to be the ringer. If it gets ugly, you're the cleanup. I won't talk to you till after the meet. Hunter, our local guy, will call you and give you the drop and roll place, because it might change after the meet."

Freddy just says okay and hangs up. He knows what's needed and is cool under fire. Now to call Rick the Stick.

The phone rings eight times, and he finally answers. "What!"

"It's your hunting buddy! You ready?"

"Go."

"Mercury Chophouse in four hours. Everything inside the place is ours, anything outside is yours. The drop and roll is at Fred's, unknown time, but I'm going to try to make it tonight."

"Got it." He hangs up.

I get a kick that all Rick needs is the locations and rules. He handles all the rest. It took me years to learn how he talks—

where, when, and the job. I have some time to run through this fiasco in my mind.

Time to call El Teco on the location we picked for the meet. That might give me an insight on El Teco's mindset. Be careful with smiles and backslaps. They will probably come in flanking the tables, three to five strong inside and the same outside. El Teco will probably sit across the table from me to show he's in charge. Paco and Rigo will have the room if it plays out the way I hope. Our ringer will have our back. Anything outside, I'm not worried—Rick the Stick has them dead to rights outside.

I will have to give El Teco his time to run his mouth and keep him thinking he has the upper hand. It's like when two fighters face off the day before the fight—all show and no go, I hope. The secret is to let whatever he says slide off my back. This meet is about learning what is in his head.

The German gave me orders to wait till tomorrow to do the drop and roll. I'm not going to wait. I am going to roll on it tonight at Fred's Cafe off Seventh Street. It's the perfect place for the drop and roll. Not only do we have South Texas boys working in the kitchen and bartending, it also open to the west. Plenty of parking garages and rooftops for Rick the Stick to speak from the clouds with his .308 rifle. I have a bad feeling we will need him to go to work. The back door is facing the northeast corner, and I assume El Teco and his boys will own it. Freddy might have to apron up again. The outside patio has a bar at the far south of the room. If I can place El Teco and his boys there, we will own them. Chiquita will have to position herself after she eyeballs the room. Simple, if it all falls in place.

What are we supposed to bring back to the German, and why is it so important to him and the cartel? They could have had El Teco bring them their prize. The money drop is the easy part. There has to be a reason other than the pinche drop we are being hired to do. The German had to know we would figure this out. He was probably counting on us to know this shit stinks to high heaven. We have to be tied to something in the mix.

Shit, who's calling me? "Who the fuck is this?"

21

CHOPHOUSE

"Okay boys, let's suit up for the meet."

"Toño, you figure anything new on this hunt?"

"We have the ringer in the kitchen and the Stick on the glass outside. They will probably wait for us to get there first, so, Paco, you take my left—yes, my left by the window. Rigo, you take my right. And, Jay, you have the bar. They will have some Rock Island Boys sit with you."

"How do you know that, Toño?"

"Rigo, look at Jay. He's the only one of us who actually looks like a natural-born killer. Plus, their young lowriders will show a true pachuco some respect. Whatever El Teco or his crew say, don't say shit. We need them to tell us everything they know through words and gestures."

"What if they start to yank and pop?"

"Then we kill them, Rigo, every one of them. The exit is to the right behind the bar. Zack always keeps it unlocked. We go down the stairs and out the back door. Rigo, you will have the football. We can't leave it behind. We all good?"

I get nods. They're frosty and ready.

I make the call to the Rock Island Boys. It takes me five minutes to have them agree to meet us; they were ready to move or they would have changed the time. We are as ready as we can be.

Jay grabs the keys, we double-check our hardware, and we're off on the trot.

"Let's show them how we do things in South Texas. Rigo, I'm serious—don't let them piss you off."

"Toño, I am too cool for school."

We go down the elevator and out the back of the hotel. Rigo and Paco take point and clear the back alley.

"All good, let's roll."

Jay gets the truck ready to move, unlocked and running. The alley is quiet and lonely and cold. Jay gives us a nod and we make a dash and load up. We scamper out and do several heat runs around the downtown area to see who might be following us. We notice a black Dodge Charger on our tail. Let's drag them to the meet.

We pull up to the Mercury Chophouse valet and I hand him a hundred-dollar bill. "This truck doesn't move from this spot."

The poor valet watches the four horsemen roll out of the truck like death has come to call.

"Keys, sir?" the valet asks with a crackling voice.

"Keys? You don't need no stinking keys," Jay whispers.

Rigo looks at Jay and smarts off. "I thought it was badges, not keys?"

"Fuck you, Rigo."

"Line up, boys, we are being watched."

Paco and Rigo are one and two, I'm sitting third, and Jay's in the rear. We all put our backs to the wall and just stand real still. Once I think they have had an eyeful, I blurb, "EPP." Nice and easy, we walk into the Mercury Chophouse. Paco and Rigo break right and left and I walk straight in, casing the restaurant and bar.

The owner, Zack the Moroccan, gives me a nod and looks to the back of the restaurant. I look over his shoulder and notice Freddy wearing a stupid hairnet. Freddy looks up just enough to let me know he's none too happy. I give Rigo a look, and he slides in with Paco to his right, running two. I slide in third, and Jay moves to the bar.

Boom—the clown and his court are sitting at the table, six strong. They're gathered around El Teco, at what was supposed to be my seat, and two more soldiers come around the back corner behind us. I look back at Jay and he has the company of two lowriders wearing the traditional khakis, white t-shirts, and flannel shirts wrapped around their right hands. Paco and Rigo back up and cover the left and right of the room. Time to focus on El Teco and what he has to say.

"Mind if I sit down?"

El Teco, sitting in my seat, has an "I got your ass" look on his tattooed face. These guys must all shop at the same Target. White t-shirts, khakis, with every part of skin that's inked out showing. El Teco looks away like he's bored and hand gestures to the chair across the table from him. Paco and Rigo are bladed and ready, covering their half of the room.

"The only reason I agreed to meet your stupid ass after you disrespected me is because the German himself asked me to."

What is that old saying—you lie to me once, you're a liar…? The German wouldn't ask this chump personally unless he was keeping something from the Mexican Cartel. Let's let this clown talk himself to death.

"This is a courtesy, but now you're in my town. You and your backward-ass fools are children dealing with men." El Teco looks at his boys, nodding and smiling, getting the same from these numbskulls. If they only knew their best scenario is to not make a play, and their worst is they all get dead.

As El Teco goes on running his head with how good they are, I'm looking around the room. Every one of his soldiers has their pistol in the front of their pants with their t-shirts over them—no holstered weapons. We have ours high on our hips, the same place we've always put them since we started this life. We practice on speed and accuracy. Plus, these city boys might shoot, what, maybe two to five times a year? We grew up shooting thousands of rounds in the ranches. Let's not forget, we have a ringer in the kitchen. No, these chumps are cooked. They just don't know it.

"And another thing, putos, you show us some respect, or I'll bury all you river rats."

I give El Teco a very small nod of understanding.

"Look at these wetback ranch hands. You're hey boys, not big noises like everybody says. I heard about your bullshit play with the cartel. You try that shit with us and it's your ass, you hear me, putos? Hey, you—you hear me, rat?"

He had to mess with Rigo. I can feel Rigo tense up, and just before he tells this homeboy to go fuck himself, I jump in.

"We hear you. You done?"

"Give me the case."

"Let's set the drop and roll time to do just that. Then, you can give me the package I came for."

"Give me the case."

"I don't have it, and, even if I did, I wouldn't give it up until I got the German's package."

"Give me the case, or you all die right here, right now, you country-ass putos!"

Death is visiting, and all it needs is a whisper.

"Teco! You really think we would bring the case with us? You think we're stupid?"

He gestures at Rigo. "It's right there, I can see it."

"What, that? Shit, it's for show. If we hadn't brought it, you would be tearing up our hotel room as we speak, now wouldn't you?"

El Teco leans back in his chair like a guy that just got played. It makes sense to him. Who would bring the money to a meet? But he's just not sure. "Then give me the case, if it ain't got nothing in it, homes. Give it to me!"

El Teco's boys start for the reach.

"EPP." Paco and Rigo draw and point. Jay doesn't move as long as his boys stay calm. Time stops. They know any movement and we will rattle off twenty rounds before they clear their khakis. I lean forward to make sure El Teco understands my intention.

"Mira, Teco, it's a fifty-fifty shot the money is in the case. We can all start spraying and praying and end up dead and empty handed. Now, it might seem you have us, but it just looks that way."

"We don't work for anybody but ourselves. You got that, river rat? The Mexican Cartel, El Commandante, and that fucking German can go to hell. We are the kings now."

"Yeah, okay, Fred's Texas Cafe in six hours. Bring the German's package or you and your clan will have to deal with his mercs."

"I'll bury him."

"Bring the package and I will bring the real case and we will make the exchange. And by the way, my name is Toño—try not to forget it. Fred's Texas Cafe in six hours." I get up from the chair and El Teco pops up from his seat with the gun he's had in hand the whole time.

"You try any of your South Texas tricks with me and you die."

As I walk off with Rigo and Paco trailing behind, I remind Rigo to grab the suitcase and say it has my underwear in it. Rigo takes it and we peel off. Jay falls behind us, covering our back. We move out the front door with nobody trailing us. We calmly get in our truck and drive off nice and easy back to the Ashton.

"See, I told you guys this would be a cakewalk."

Dead silence crowds us, as the sticky stillness grabs ahold.

"What just happened inside that deathtrap?"

"Let's just get back to the room, Paco. We still have to stay frosty."

Two minutes later, Jay backs up the truck at the Ashton and we line up all the way back to the room. As soon as the door shuts, it starts all at once.

"What the fuck?"

"Did you see those crazy dudes?"

"How did we get out of that rat trap?"

"Toño, what was all that shit about the case being a switch?"

"You like that, Paco? That's all I had, and I had to sell it, or we would have been off to the races."

"Why did you bring it? You slipped, Toño."

"Maybe, Jay, but where would you have stashed our lives? Because we lose that case, we are dead. It's better with us than in the wind. I was just hoping he would be professional and run the game like we had drafted it."

"I didn't like the way they talked to us. I'd rather yank and pop those pinche city boys than put up with being disrespected." Paco says.

The room goes quiet. It's not often Paco speaks; even less often like that. Paco is always smiling and will divulge bits and pieces of what he's thinking. This, he meant. If I don't deal with him right now, he is capable of walking to Rock Island and pulling a *Scarface*.

"Paco, how many of these sits have we been through? How many times have we dealt with these doped-up chumps constantly farting out of their mouth? I know you were pissed when he fucked with Rigo, your own brother. I really thought Rigo was going to rattle off a bunch of fuck yous and kiss my asses."

Paco cracks a smile and lets out a laugh. "Toño, remember what you told that cowboy from the King Ranch in Kingsville? 'Hey, sonny, didn't your mother ever teach you not to break wind out of your mouth?' And his mother was sitting behind him? That was embarrassing."

"Paco, I get it, but we got a lot from this meet besides our lives."

"I missed all that shit. Catch me up."

"I'm glad you weren't with us in the back, Jay. Your pachuco blood would be boiling."

"Toño, these guys are all show. They don't know what they are doing."

"How you know that, Jay?"

"Listen, Rigo, and learn. The two guys up at the bar were wearing fucked-up tats. They weren't jailhouse; they were like kids' names. One even had a Dallas Cowboys tat. Then, they had their revolvers wrapped up in flannel shirts."

"You're right, Jay."

"What does that have to do with anything, Toño?"

"Think about it. Revolvers have hammers. You cover the hammer with the shirt, and it won't cock and fire. No wonder you didn't yank, Jay."

"I had them cold."

"Okay, Toño, what else did you pick up in the meet? We were too busy watching their hands and eyes."

True villains are always watching their eyes and hands. The eyes always give you away. When you start to look around and make a move, you always squint. You can't help it. If you can spot it early, you have the edge."

"Well, guys, we know they think they're smarter than we are."

"How the hell you pick that up?"

162

"Rigo, you're the youngest, but you have to start paying attention. They arrived early and set up in a way they thought would have us in a barrel. But they didn't plan on a ringer, and they don't know shit about weapons or how to carry them."

"I saw how they were wearing their guns, up front and covered. I knew we had them on the jump."

"Good eye, Rigo, but El Teco was the unknown. He always kept one hand under the table. I figured he had to have a pistol. He was mine to handle."

"He would have been hard to beat, Toño."

"I would have had to outlast him until one of you guys made a canoe of his head. Now, the Pelican suitcase—all that Teco wants is the case. If we hadn't set up right, he would have made a play for it. I put enough doubt in his mind for him to back off."

The thing that worried me more was the package we're supposed to collect and bring back. When I mentioned it to El Teco, he looked confused. Either he doesn't have it or it's not a package. And, lastly, why would they think they could do business off or around the cartel? They are either so fucked up on their own shit, or they somehow have leverage. He actually said we will bury "him," not "them." That didn't sound right. Hell, that might be the voodoo shit this clown thinks will protect him.

I saw the cartel handle a guy like him in Matamoros, Mexico. "You guys remember the Paleros doing all that Palo Mayombe shit?" I take a moment to see if my boys are with me. They are sitting around like kids watching soft porn. "Well, the main guy thought he was invincible, making noise about the cartel just like Teco. The cartel soldiers snatched him and, several days later, that Palero showed up in the main plaza of Matamoros. The cartel butcher cut his arms and legs off, but that wasn't enough. They took his eyes and tongue. They sat him in a wheelchair by the fountain, still alive. That's how El Tony came into power—they had an opening."

"You know, Toño, we didn't have to hear that story."

"The point is, Rigo, this crew has a short life in front of them."

"So, what? You got me all fucked up in the head. Why are we here, or do they have something the cartel and the German want? That makes no sense. They can come and drop these fools. But to retrieve what they want, they need talent, not muscle. The cartel doesn't come out this far unless it's a quick hit and run—that's why they need us. We are the retrievers, and damn good at it."

"Bingo, Jay! They can't get what they want. They need slick villains like us to get them their prize."

"What do you think, Toño? Diamonds, gold, season tickets to the Cowboys?"

"Paco, what do you think the cartel, El Commandante, and the German all fear the most?"

He leans in.

"Information."

22

I WOKE UP TWICE

I woke up twice today. The cartel wants something or somebody and are scared of it being out in the open. I feel like the dog finally caught the car and doesn't know what to do with it. Jay hands me the clean phone; I need to call Paesan.

The phone rings ten times before he picks it up. "Yo, who the fuck is this?"

"It's the big bad wolf, you toilet-swinging Yankee."

"Toño, why you calling? You guys in the wind already?"

"No, where is Roberto right now?"

"I'm looking right at him. He's all over Chiquita at the bar."

"What bar?"

"Downtown at Del Frisco's—not the bullshit grill, but the old one."

"Hey, I like that place. It's really badass."

"What the fuck do you want? She hasn't broken free to tell me shit yet."

"Get a hold of Hunter. Does he have that bigshot attorney that has contacts outside the country?"

"Who, Benson the Barbarian?"

"Yeah, tell Hunter I need him to make someone disappear. I know he owes you guys, so I'll cover his debt plus throw him 20 percent of what we take in on this job."

Benson the Barbarian is a high-priced lawyer who's lived all over the world. He always takes care of the worst and comes out on top. He's stocky and always wears a beard. I'm not sure where he is from, but he can pass for Mexican. You ever need an attorney, you bring in the best, and that's Benson the Barbarian. He sucks at cards, though; the only thing Benson hates more than shaving is letting go of his money. Hunter calls him "Benson One Time" because he only picked up the check one time in his life.

"Paesan, tell him I need Benson with a passport and fake ID for one tonight. Put a gun to his head if you have to."

"I got it, Toño. He'll be there one way or another."

"Get Hunter up and running, and this is what I want you guys and Chiquita to do…."

23

THE SETUP

It's time to set the stage, one that will work in our favor. We will be outmanned, but not outgunned. Time to call for help.

Rick the Stick picks up the phone on the first ring. "What?"

"I need you to bring a spare long rifle and get my boy, Freddy, on the glass. I need him covering us at the drop and roll. You need to cover Freddy—they'll have their guy on a scope, so you need to find him and drop the hammer. Dangle Freddy as bait."

"Okay, talk to me."

"Freddy is 6'2", 235 pounds, all muscle, clean-shaven. Looks like a big ass Tom Cruise with Cher's hair from the seventies.

"What the fuck—"

"Trust me. He's a big hunter, so he knows long rifles better than most. Give Freddy the location you want him to set up, and don't make it too obvious. Pick him up in thirty minutes outside Zack's Chophouse."

Rick just hangs up. Now to call Freddy and give him the change of plans. "Freddy, where are you?"

"Zack's. He's feeding me a killer steak."

"Rick the Stick will pick you up there in thirty minutes, so don't eat too much. I need you on the quick. He will have a long rifle for you to cover us. Listen to Rick—he will give you your spot. Freddy, don't freelance. Stay where he tells you. He will have your back, I give you my word."

"Fuck it, anything is better than being in the kitchen wearing that stupid hairnet."

"Thank Zack for me. I'll get with him later. Freddy, I'm counting on you."

"Kiss my ass, I will be there, just as always."

The killing is in play and the dice are rolling. Let's play this out. I can't see how we avoid shooting our way out of this one. They will be in front of us just like the O.K. Corral. They aren't smart enough to use cover or concealment. Paco and Rigo can take three each. I will be out in the open, so I can hit at least two before I get cut down.

It has to do with information—what else could it be? El Teco got his hands on something that makes him think he is untouchable. Not something, but someone that can cripple the cartel. But why all the shroud around the German? Why did I meet the German in Guerrero, a neutral place the cartel never uses? He only used his mercs in the meet, no cartel boys. All the heat runs for a bullshit meet. Why? Was the German hiding from the Federales, or—

The German!

24

THE GERMAN

"That slick, well-dressed fucking German."

Rigo and Paco run into the bedroom, yelling, "Where?"

"Let's go in the parlor for a powwow, but let me call Hunter first." He answers on the first ring. I guess all of us are up and ready for the fiasco. "Hunter, I need you to find the Farrier and have him bring some C4 with a control for a lining.

Yes, he will know what I'm talking about. I need it in the next hour. Good luck on your end. Bye."

I put down the phone and turn to my crew. "You're not going to believe what I am going to lay on you."

"Toño, we're in no motherfucking mood to play twenty questions, homeboy. Just tell us we're gonna be alive tomorrow."

"Jay, you're old school, you will love it. I'm going to lay out how we are going to beat the beast."

I lay out the situation and the plan to the guys. As uncomfortable and crazy as it is, they buy into it. They don't really have a choice—sort of like when a gambler is pot committed in a poker hand. They have too much invested to walk away. Plus, it's a great plan, if I say so myself.

The Ferrier arrives and we go to work.

"Rigo, is the case ready?"

"Yeah, but I don't have a master lock to replace the one I cut off."

"Farrier, you have any superglue?"

"No, but I have quick dry cement. I use it for split wood on stocks and grips."

"Put it on the lock, Rigo, and let it set. All it has to do is hold long enough."

"I hope you're right, Toño."

176

"Okay, the devil is loose. Let's see whose side he's on tonight."

We all load up and get ready for a game of chess with checkers players.

"Jay, tie up the Farrier. We can't afford to let our plan leak out, or it's adiós, muchachos!"

Jay hogties the old man. "Sorry about this."

The old man knows we could just shoot him, so he doesn't complain. Truth of the matter is, we really aren't cold-blooded killers. But people don't need to know that. I've always said we're a ten-dollar pair of boots with a hundred-dollar shine.

"Jay, take the Farrier's cellphone and tear room phones out of the wall. This old man probably has more tricks up his sleeve. And stick a towel in his mouth."

"I won't say anything, I give you my word."

"I can't give you the opportunity. Be glad we don't just ghost you."

The old man complies, but he is none too happy about the towel in the mouth.

"Toño, you think of everything."

I smile at Rigo. "You bet your ass." For the first time in this backstabbing bullshit job, I can see the sense in the game.

There's a knock at the door—the man we've been expecting has arrived. Jay reluctantly opens it, and there he is in all his glory—Benson the Barbarian.

"Can I come in, or is this a bad time?"

"Benson, you carpetbagger, come on in."

"What on earth can I do for you, Toño? You paid my debt, and for that, I thank you. It was also brought to my attention that a 20-percent rate was to come my way, but of how much?"

"I need you to hold onto money for me. Your 20 percent is from this pile. If we don't make it, send this money to the address in the bag with this letter. You try to sweeten your end or try a fast one, I will have Freddy visit you wherever you go."

"Freddy...he should be the one called the Barbarian. I will honor my end of the deal."

"I like your style. Guys like you *do* grow on trees. Don't forget the papers for our out-of-town guest."

"Consider it done, Toño. He will be in the proverbial wind by morning. And with that, I bid you gentlemen adiós."

And just like that, the money in the case is out of our reach. For a good reason.

"You know the game and you know your places, so let's dance. Rigo, be real careful with that suitcase."

We walk to the elevator, looking at our reflections on the brass doors. All at the same time, we fix our hair and tuck and shift. Have to look good on the hustle. If everything goes to plan, by the time we get to the drop and roll, we will have a ten-yard lead on the run to the end zone.

25

THE DROP AND ROLL

Rolling up to Fred's, I can tell something is wrong—not one car in the front parking lot. I know it's late, but usually there's at least one or two barflies hanging on till the last beer is poured. I look at my crew; they look edgy, but cool and calm. Sort of like the look Cool Hand Luke would give you. You can't tell what they're thinking.

"Toño, any place special?"

"First spot left of the front door. Let's go in the patio, toward the back bar."

"There's nobody here. No bartenders or waitresses."

"What did you expect, a marching band? Paco, let's do the circle and wherever they crawl out, we'll horseshoe them in. Jay, the back is yours. Don't let them do a creep up on our backside."

Here come three black Suburbans, pulling up right in front. Twelve Rock Island Boys carrying MAC-10s and MP5 submachine guns—they mean business tonight. They break up outside the patio, four outside on the south side. The other eight come up in front of us, pointing barrels and looking nervous. El Teco steps out of the middle SUV and does a slow, homerun strut toward us. He stops in the middle of his clowns, rubbing his hands together and smiling.

"Give me the case, ese, or I will blow you to hell!"

"Where's my package?"

"It's in the middle car, you want to see him?"

"The only person you could have that the German has been looking for is my tio and fat Machete. And you don't have the smarts to put your hands on the big prize the cartel's been looking for. Or do you?" I say this with a smile. I knew it was my tio, and thank god Teco didn't pull a fast one and just kill him. My plans would have turned to shit in a handbasket.

"I got your fucking uncle when he walked right into my bar, El Arbolito. He told me a story. That's why you're here, and that's why I have the German on the dangle."

"My tio, El Maestro, is alive? You're telling me he just walked into your bar and gave up all the information? Let me guess, it was about cocaine that was stolen from the cartel."

"He is alive for now," El Teco spits out. "You're supposed to cut off his hand before you kill him. That's the box you take back."

"Proof of death, huh. Have your homeboy turn the dome light on so I can see him."

"Okay," El Teco says with a smile. "Prende la luz!"

The driver in the middle car turns the interior light on. Sure as hell and bigger than life, there is my tio with duct tape wrapped around his mouth, all back of the bus and shit! I start laughing. "You guys see him all taped up and shit?"

My crew starts to laugh and point at his backstabbing ass.

"What's so funny, putos?"

"Sorry, Teco, but look at him. It's funny, dude."

El Teco looks back and starts to chuckle himself. "He is funny, right."

"Change of plans, Teco. I can't give you the case. It goes to somebody else. But I will give you somebody in trade that's worth more than gold."

Right about then, a white Range Rover pulls up and gets five gun barrels pointed at it by the Rock Island Boys.

"Be cool, Teco, because I am going to save your life tonight." I nod, and the back window rolls down. And, there, a hooded dude sits. "You know who that is?"

He looks at me with fear in his eyes. "Roberto?"

Inside the Range Rover are three kidnappers with their faces covered by bandanas. One pulls off the hood and exposes El Teco's weak spot.

"You hurt him, and I'll kill all you motherfuckers!"

"What's more important—the money, or the life of your brother?"

"What do you want?"

"What do I want?"

"What do you want, Toño?"

"You see, you can remember my name. I need you to hold off the German mercs long enough to get my tio in that Range Rover and to safety."

"The German! Here?"

"Teco, he's been here the whole time."

"Bullshit, I would have known."

"Do we have a deal? I give you my word I will let Roberto go after we leave. Unlike you, I keep my word, and this you know."

"Yes," El Teco whispers with his head down. He's whipped.

"Circle your boys between my tio's car and the Rover. I want him covered all the way to the car."

El Teco turns around and yells out to his guys, "You heard him! Cover a path for that old man to the Rover, a la volada!"

The gauntlet is set. My tio steps out of the SUV, still taped up. He looks directly at me and then up to the sky. I nod at him, letting him know I have it covered. I can see the relief in his body language. As my tio is walking from the Suburban, we hear a rifle shot ring out. Everybody drops their heads two inches, except for my tio. The master of the game, he knew I had it covered. My kidnappers in the Range Rover—Chiquita, Hunter, and Paesan—drag Roberto over to the middle seat, load my tio, and off they go.

"You got what you wanted. Now, when and where are you going to let my brother go?"

"The game is just starting. Jay, do you see them?"

"Yeah, they're coming from the northwest by the covered parking lot."

Eight suited mercs surround the slim-figured German himself, who's walking with his hands behind his waist like he doesn't have a care in the world.

"Teco, don't do anything stupid. I outplayed you. Now, I'm going to outplay the fucking German, and you're part of it. They'll be writing songs about you, homeboy."

"Okay, do your thing, Toño. I'll play off you. Just don't fuck me." El Teco likes the sound of that.

The mercs set up where it's useless for any of us to resist. They're all packing high-capacity, fully auto M-16 assault rifles with double-stack magazines. They could mow us down within seconds, but I have an ace in the hole. At least, I hope I do.

The German walks up, wearing a beautiful, black suit with a royal blue shirt and an open collar.

"What, no tie today, German?"

"You should hire better snipers, little Toño. Your little deer hunter will not match up with my highly trained killers."

"You took out my sniper? No fucking way, you fucking German bastard!"

"Joe, please show this river rat some manners."

"My old friend, Joe, we meet again."

As Joe starts to close in, I point at a Lone Star sign next to me. A rifle shot rings out, and a hole the size of a 110-grain bullet appears right in the middle of the sign.

"Stop!" the German yells. He looks at Joe. "I thought you took care of the pesky sniper, yes?"

Just about then, the German looks at me and says in a different tone, "Ah, you had two pesky snipers? Clever boy."

Imagine that—I have the German on the dangle, out in the open, exposed.

"It might seem like you have the advantage, Toño, but it just seems that way."

I can see the German sweating and fidgeting around. I got him, I got the unbeatable, and he knows it.

"Listen to me, Toño. We want your uncle, and if you deliver him, we will grant you a pass for this indiscretion."

"Who is 'we'? You fucking psycho! There is no 'we'! You fucked the cartel by keeping all the cocaine my tio stole, and as long as he's alive, your little secret's in play.

"El Teco nabbed my tio here in Fort Worth where he was hiding, and my tio tells him all about the cocaine you decided to keep from the cartel. So, they blackmail the famous German, and that doesn't sit right with you, does it? You can't afford to have El Teco and his crew staying alive, so you cook up a story and send us in to kill my new friends in Rock Island. Then, all you have to do is kill any survivors at the drop and roll.

"It all looks like a deal gone bad, and you're back in the clear with the cartel. I really thought you would send your boy,

Joe, and the gang, but why did you come? You must be pretty worried about the cartel."

"I always said, didn't I, Joe, we must keep an eye on this one, clever boy. I have a place for you and your crew, when and only when you bring me my prize."

"You believe this guy, Teco?"

"Toño, you got balls. You and your crew can hang out with the Rock Island Boys anytime, ese."

"Look, German, I have you and you know it. I know your boys can chop us down easy, but in any scenario you can think of, you die. My sniper has you dead to rights, and he's the best."

"Ah, you have the Rick? I should have known something was amiss when I could not find him for this job."

"Face it, German, they like me more than they fear you. That's the difference between us. Your days are numbered, so if I was you, I would go back to whatever town you're from and change your name. I would think the cartel wants to have a word with you. Can you imagine dying on the streets of Fort Worth? I mean what could be worse, ay comrade?"

The German starts to look around, searching for any way out.

"Listen, Mr. German, my tio stays in the wind, and now we—you and me and Teco—have this little secret. I won't say a word about this. How about you, Teco?"

"Me, I won't tell more than three people."

"See, so go in peace, slick. Rigo, bring up the case. Here you go, German. I don't know what's in the case, but I doubt it's money. I think it's full of phonebooks, and when El Teco opened it, the war would start. Take your shit, bounce, and live to bother us another day. Joe, maybe next time you and I will scrap?"

Joe looks at me with disbelief. "I hope to never see you again."

The German grabs the case, looking like he just aged ten years. "I will find your uncle, then you, my petulant boy. I will take my time teaching you about your betters." He turns, with the mercs covering him to the parking lot from which they came.

I raise my hands so nobody makes any moves. "Rigo, let's wait until you hear the doors slam and the bees are in the butter."

Rigo blurts out our go word, "EPP!"

The next thing we hear is an explosion from the parking lot. Boom, you're dead, German!

"I guess that cement held. So long, German, and vaya con el diablo, motherfucker! What do think of that, Teco?"

He gives me a hug. "Dude, I want to be on your side from now on."

I drag my hand across my chest, letting Freddy and Rick the Stick know the job is over and it's time to bug out. I get on the phone and Chiquita answers. "Let Roberto out at the Ashton. We're all on our way there for a pachanga."

I hang up and turn to the others. "What say we all pack our shit away, head to the Ashton, and take over the bar? Teco, you mind having one of your boys go collect the German's hand?" I will have to explain to the cartel what the pinche German was up to, and they will want confirmation.

"You got it. I'll have it boxed for you."

"Vironga time, compadres!"

We all load up and head to the Ashton for some R&R. My crew is just quiet and stunned.

"Well, boys, how did you like that, huh?"

"Dude, it was like watching a movie. I still can't believe my eyes."

"I know, right? I can't either, but we did it. Truth be told, I got a phone call that the German was seen at the Four Seasons in Las Colinas."

"Who called you?"

"El Machete called me, can you believe it? A blast from the past. My tio's right-hand man calls me with the German's location. My tio probably set this whole thing up back before he escaped the German and the Mexican Cartel. He knew the German kept the cocaine, so he began to set up this whole scam. Why do you think he walked into El Arbolito bar and turned himself over to El Teco? He played us all like the master he is at the smuggler's game."

"You knew about your tio? That's why you brought Benson in the picture. Why didn't you tell us? That was low, Toño."

"I couldn't take the chance, Rigo. You guys would have thought twice about going to the drop and roll. Jay, if you had known we were making an exchange for my tio, would you have gone? If you guys knew the German was making a play to kill us all, would you have gone? I had to keep this information close to the vest for your own good. It was a shitty thing to do to my own crew, but remember, I was standing next to you in the play. I wouldn't ask you to do anything I wouldn't do myself."

"Fuck you, Toño. Not telling us is the same as lying."

"Jay, you really want to know what I have to do or the details of each job? Do you really want to know all the preparations and plans I have to line up? You guys want to know how we ended up in Yucatan alive after the drag we did in Mexico? My tio set it up. He set up the transportation in Mexico and the place we stayed in. He did this because I gave him the heads up the cartel was on their way to kill him and fat Machete. He had already figured it out, but he helped us out. At the end of the day, blood is still blood.

"Paco, you think I would fuck you guys over money or my tio?"

"I know you wouldn't play us just to save your tio because I know we are family. What you said is true—I wouldn't have gone to the drop and roll if I knew it was for your pinche tio. I also know if we hadn't gone, the German would have had us killed, and where would we be? You played the right hand on our behalf."

"You think so, Paco? Toño lied to us, and you think he did it for our benefit? Fuck that shit, I'm done with this crew. You all can go to fucking hell. If you don't like it, make a move, homeboys."

Steady, boys. We are not going to start killing ourselves after the play we just made on the German.

"I get it, Jay. You're the best villain I have ever had the pleasure of working with. This isn't blood in, blood out. You can leave anytime you want. I know you wanted to leave before this gig, and I thank you for coming. Now, you will have enough of the German's money to get that place in Monterrey you're always talking about."

"I'm serious. I'm really pissed off at all you assholes."

Paco and Rigo start to chuckle in the back of the truck, and then we all start to laugh with a sigh of relief. Jay can't keep a straight face and joins in, even as he's still telling us how mad he is. Jay wants to retire, and he just didn't know how to say or do it. So, he played the mad soldier rebelling. He knows I wouldn't fuck him; if he did, he would just pop me with his Colt Python pistol.

"Toño, did they kill Freddy?"

"No way, Paco. I had Rick the Stick use Freddy as bait, but don't tell him. Freddy will kill my ass if he finds out I dangled him. Rick was countering their sniper, so the German thought his guy took ours out. He made his worst mistake—he didn't double-check. He just assumed. You assume, you make an ass out of you and me, get it?"

"How did you know he would take the case back?"

"Have you not been watching, Rigo? The German tells us the case is full of money, knowing we probably would think it wasn't. Either way, he assumed we wouldn't open it up to check. I'm glad we did that lookie-loo back in Zapata, or else we would have been in bad shape. So, after knowing the German's play, we lined the case with the C4 the Farrier brought us and cemented the lock in hopes the German would not notice we had cut it off. That German had planned to get his money back after the killings. Would you leave this much money behind?"

"Now what, Toño?"

"We go to the Ashton and drink with our new friends. Let's all stay frosty and keep your guns close, just in case Teco changes his mind."

We pull up to the Ashton and park out back. A dark Lincoln creeps up with the driver's side window down. I tell the boys I'll see them inside. I have business I need to finish.

Benson the Barbarian is behind the wheel. "Hello, Toño. I see you made it in one piece." He hands me the bag of money I had him hold for us. "I took my 20 percent to move your guy out of the country."

"Benson, if you took more than your cut, I will send Freddy to your house on Sunday while you're having dinner and he will throw you a South Texas horse whipping with a knotted plowline."

Benson takes a moment and then pulls out ten grand from his coat pocket. "Sorry, I couldn't help it."

I lean in and catch a glimpse of my tio, a man I used to think of as my father, my blood. "Tio, this is twice I have saved your life. First was the phone call that the cartel and El Commandante were coming to kill you, and now this."

"You saved me? I think you have it backwards. The only reason you and your crew are still alive is because of me. If I hadn't played the German and put you guys in the know, he would have had you in the barrel, dead to rights."

"I see it different, Tio, but it doesn't matter now. You have your life back."

"Toño, you have become the best I have ever seen. You're welcome. Now, I can relax in my old age, and we are even."

I lean back and throw Benson the ten grand. "Give this to that man in the backseat when you set him up wherever. I don't ever want to see you again, Tio. You're way too much trouble."

I head wave Benson and off they go. Despite my words, I have a bad feeling we shall cross paths again in the future.

All I have to do now is convince the Mexican Cartel what game the German was up to and deliver the proof of death. Easier said than done.

My tio died with the German in that parking lot in Fort Worth. That's the story and we're sticking to it.

I walk into the Ashton and see nothing but smiles lined up across the bar. Freddy the Saint is arguing with Rick the Stick about being used as bait. Rick is just standing with a Coors in his hand, completely ignoring Freddy's rant. Rigo and Paco are giving Teco a class on how to carry handguns and set up a room on a meet. Chiquita and Snow White are sharing clothing tips while Roberto is staring at them like a wolf eyeing rabbits—but everyone knows it's the other way around. I walk up to Hunter and Paesan, who are always standing at the end of the bar, where the money is.

"Toño, it's always a pleasure working with a true professional."

'Thank you, Hunter. We couldn't have done it without you and Paesan. I'll have your cut before you leave tonight."

"I'm going to stand right here with the money if you don't mind."

"Why would I, Paesan? Just don't sneak up behind me with a toilet seat."

"Yo, it was a toilet lid, not a seat. Everybody gets it fucking wrong, you know?"

The money is in good hands, but I still give Rigo a nod to watch the bag. If you don't leave anything to chance, chance won't take anything from you. I walk over to Snow White and Chiquita. I put my arms around them and say, "Just because you dance with the devil, doesn't mean you have to let him lead."

THE END

About the Author & Co.

TONY MOLINA was born in Laredo and grew up in the small town of Zapata, Texas where most of his writing inspirations derived. Tony's second book is a sequel to his Amazon bestselling debut novel, *South Texas Drag*.

In *South Texas Twist*, Book II of the Smuggler's Tales, the author delivers a unique flavor for the smuggler's way of life. Tony moved his cast of groovy characters from Book I to Fort Worth to set the stage. This city is where he spent twenty-seven years as an Arlington Texas police officer, a vice/narcotic's detective, a SWAT team member (thirteen years), and a detective sergeant until retirement. He knows it well.

As a unique way of celebrating the priceless friendships he's made on and off the job throughout the decades, and as a *thank you* for their love and loyalty, Tony has fashioned many of the characters in his books after the friends in the photos that follow....

Author Tony Molina with Randle "Hunter" Meadows, Joey "Paesan" Garofano, and Robert "Roberto the Shark" Rivera

Tony Molina with his friend Rick "The Stick" Wade, PhD

Riitta "Snow White" Klint at Artist Riitta Klint studio in Miami, Florida

Elizabeth "Chiquita" DeLeon Bennett, retired Arlington Police detective
(She was with author Tony Molina back in the narcotics days….)

Ramiro "Ito" Torres ~
R.I.P.

Norma "La Changa"
Ramirez, Zapata resident

Hamid "Zack" Sekouri, owner of Mercury Chophouse, Fort Worth, Texas

Mickey Demos, owner of Mickey Demos Boxing and Fitness Gym in Miami, Florida.

Tony Molina and Peter Watson at his place in Yucatán, Mexico where it all began:
Pedro Paila Resort

Benson "The Barbarian" Varghese
Varghese Summersett PLLC Forth Worth Criminal Defense Attorney

Federico "Freddy the Saint" Salinas

Rancher, top griller and smoker, political advisor extraordinaire

Glossary

These translations can have different meanings in different parts of the world.

Chingado: Damn it

Que Paso: What's up

Jefita: Mom

Chante: Home, house

Refinar: Eat

Feria: Money

Tio: Uncle

Trompo: Top

Mirones: Onlookers,

Mesquite: Mesquite tree

Sal Si Puedes: Leave if you can

Monja: Nun

Compas: Friend

Machete: Machete, long blade

Pinsoyate: Dumbass, knucklehead

Esquina: Back up Quetes: Guns, firearms

Fila: Knife

Tiros: Bullets

Gasofa: Vehicle gas

Huevos: Balls, guts

Pendejo: Stupid, idiot

Vato and Ese: Guy, dude

Dale: Go on, let's do it, hurry up

Vales Verga: You ain't worth dick

Chingos: Many, a lot

Putas: Whores, prostitutes

Orale: Okay, it's cool

Virongas: Beers

Pinche: Cheap

Whachale: Watch out, look out

Rinches: Texas Rangers, Law Men

Vanas: Bath, shower

Chamuscando: Burning Cactus

Quetes: Pistols

Pelan los ojos: Keep an eye out

Mi Changita: My little monkey

SOUTH
TEXAS
TWIST

37736136R00132

Made in the USA
Middletown, DE
03 March 2019